RUGGED TRAILS

Two Thousand Grueling Miles Book 2

L. J. MARTIN

Published in the United States by Wolfpack Publishing, Las Vegas

Wolfpack Publishing
6032 Wheat Penny Avenue
Las Vegas, NV 89122

wolfpackpublishing.com

Paperback ISBN: 978-1-64734-004-9
eBook ISBN: 978-1-64734-003-2
Library of Congress Control Number: 2019956872

RUGGED TRAILS

1

"It ain't like you're no virgin to killing men, if'n what I hear is true. Mister Jake Zane, as I heared it, killed more'n one on the Oregon trail getting here?"

"No, sir. This Jake Zane killed only one and that was self-defense." I eye him from stem to stern, and stern he is. A hard man I'd guess from first impression, a head taller than me and me tall for my age. He's got no extra suet on him. In fact, my pa would have called him spindleshanks. Hands scarred and knotted, face pitted and lined and tanned dark like a walnut with a slash of white scar across his left eye now gone milk-white. If something about half-frightening can be called milk. Rattlesnake milk maybe. Gunter Stadt, most call him Gun, he says. And he's pressing me for an answer.

"Look, younger, you ain't comin' back this season from them locusts eatin' your wheat to chaff. It's two dollars a day plus found and mostly all you gotta do is ride shotgun from here to San Francisco. Two months at the most. Then you can hire on to a lumber ship, pile off in Portland, and catch another hitch on a river boat back to home. You'll be suppin' with your lady folk in three months. Are you with us, or not?"

"You said something about a bonus when we get there?"

"One hundred dollars in gold, you hang with us and don't show no yellow streak."

That made the heat rise in my backbone. "Mister Stadt, I may have only seventeen years but I brought my Ma and two sisters the last fifteen hundred miles here from Missouri when I had only fifteen years. A fellow with a yellow streak wouldn't a got here safe."

He gives me a big smile, showing a missing eye tooth flanked by ones gone brown. Then he laughs and slaps his thigh. His breath singes my eyes like hot burning coal oil.

"Dang if you ain't got a little sass like I was told. Can you shoot straight?"

"We ain't gone hungry these two years. And that wasn't 'cause of what we growed. Ma says I got eyes like an eagle and am fast as a rattler. You've come this far from Coeur d'Alene and only now feel the need for a shotgun guard?"

"Poor William, our guard, took ill and he's buried in yonder Lewiston cemetery. So, you see we've had one all along."

"Took ill…"

"So, are you ridin' scattergun or not?"

The fact is I've been wishing I could get to Portland as there's a girl there who gave me my first kiss on the Oregon trail. While we stayed to stake some rich land near where the Salmon joins the Snake, just upriver from Lewiston, she and her family went on to the Willamette. Portland via San Francisco is not exactly a direct route from eastern Oregon, but it's getting there. And maybe getting there with a poke full of gold. Seeing if Miss Amalie Engstrom still has eyes for me will be worth the trip—or so I hope.

So, I swallow the knot in my throat and give him a nod, with a caveat. "Mister Stadt, I'll ride along, pull my weight, and pull a trigger should it be necessary. But, sir, I hope your word is as good as the gold you say you're hauling as I'd hate to dispute a man with your reputation. But know now, I will if it comes to that."

He laughs again, a deep guffaw, and sticks out a gnarled right hand. "Dang if you ain't full of piss and vinegar. We'll be headin' out come first light. Bring your own bedroll and personals."

We shake, his grip like the bite of one of my old mules. Then as I mount my Sand Bay, I realize I'm clamping my jaw. What the devil have I done?

I've said my goodbyes to Sampson, the escaped slave Pa hired on before we left Missouri and my good friend, and his wife Mary who he met on the trail; to my older sister Edna Mae, her husband Twist, my baby niece, and eighteen-old nephew; to my little sister Willy, Wilhelmina, who just turned fifteen; and the most difficult goodbye of all to my Ma. I'm happy she has taken Captain Quinton Haroldson as husband. With him recently separated from the Army, I couldn't hope for her and the rest of my family to be in better hands. My Pa died of the cholera not long into the trip he dreamed of taking, and the country is just too difficult for a woman not to be wed to a strong man. I truly believe Sampson and Captain Haroldson could take on a band of a dozen hostiles, should it come to that.

I'd favor taking Shep, my hound, along, but feel that he'd better serve Ma and the others. Much as I figure I could use his fine hearing and nose on the trail, I have to order him to stay behind. He's proven he can sense a grizzly or a savage long before any of we weak humans know either are within a quarter mile, so it's a chore for me to say fare-thee-well.

We've worked like the four mules we now own to till, plant, and harvest the land we've claimed, but we'll have to stay on it two more years—a total of four—to get final title to our claims. The first year we did fine with wheat, corn, and garden crops. But this year, the locusts came and cleaned all down to the mud. Damn if they didn't even eat the straw off one of Ma's brooms. We took to hunting elk and selling meat to the riverboats on the Snake, trapping some beaver, coons and cats, and anything we could accomplish to keep body and soul together.

So, I couldn't turn down Mr. Gunter Stadt's offer of two dollars a day for two month's work, plus the promise of a hundred-dollar bonus should we get his cargo safe to San Francisco.

It looks to me to be a king's ransom, at the moment.

Ma has fed me a breakfast of side pork, gravy and biscuits, and I'm off for the three quarters of an hour ride, if at a canter, to meet up with Mr. Stadt and his party at Lewiston, where the Clearwater River joins the Snake.

It's dang near nine hundred miles to San Francisco from Lewiston, so I think Mr. Stadt is a mite ambitious to believe we'll make it in two months. If my cyphering is correct, two months to make nine hundred miles is fifteen miles a day. You might average that easy enough on the Oregon Trail, but much of the way south has no trail, not a two track, not much more than old Indian trading trails or even game trails. He has two freight wagons being pulled by two six-ups of mules, so he could make the speed, but not so, should he run out of road—and I know he soon will. He did say he'd go to packing the mules should he have to, and I know he'll have to. He's been wise enough to pack panniers and pack saddles and a goodly supply of hemp rope and leather latigo strapping in the wagons.

So, even though the job is riding the left wagon seat, alongside the driver, and keeping an eye out for trouble, I'm bringing my own riding horse and tack. Pa was a saddle and harness maker and I've got the best-ever leather, ever put together by homo sapiens—human hands. Pa made his own oak and hickory saddle trees and rebuilt the wagon and cart we crossed the plains and mountains with, and never a joint failed, nor did the harness. It still serves as the finest farm wagon in the territory. I'm also bringing my own weapons. Pa bought us all Colt sidearms afore we set out to Oregon, so my .44 caliber is on my hip and I have double scabbards on Sandy, my Sand Bay gelding. One carries a double-barrel scattergun in .12 gauge and one a .44 caliber muzzle loader that can trade slugs with the Colt, but with which I can consistently put slugs in a twenty-inch circle at one hundred fifty yards. My rough-out elk-hide possibles bag has balls, wads, caps, cleaning rod, and a bag of gunpowder. A generous powder horn hangs alongside full to the neck.

My haversack, tightly sewn by my sis Edna Mae from Mr. Goodyear's rubberized canvas, has seams sealed with beeswax. It carries a spare pair of canvas trousers, a linsey-woolsey shirt, a spare coat fashioned from a Hudson's Bay blanket, sox, underwear and a fine pair of moccasins from the nearby Nez Perce tribe nearly fill it. I've made friends with those handsome folks and traded venison and elk for salmon, fur, and leather goods several times. Two big elk-bull carcasses bought me the fine elk-skin fringed trousers I wear, and two more the fringed jacket. I truly believe the chief's wife—I think her name means Pretty Hawk—has taken a shine to me and helps me bargain for goods. Sacks of hardtack and jerky fill the spaces in the haversack even though I assured Ma that

Mr. Stadt was well provisioned.

My wide-brimmed, well starched canvas hat and leather boots will keep the elements off'n me.

The haversack and bedroll are a fat load on the back of Sandy. Luckily, they'll ride in the wagon. I do plan to drag him behind a wagon, but where there's any chance of mischief, he'll be saddled with both long guns scabbarded and loaded.

Stadt is camped on the west side of the Snake, so I don't have to cross. As Sandy picks his way down the steep slope, I can see the five men I'm to accompany are dousing fires and sucking up latigos on three of six saddle horses—three to ride and three spares, as two of the five I'm to join will be on wagon seats for at least the beginning of our journey. The twelve mules are in harness, two six-up teams. The sun is still well below the crown of the mountains to the east, so I'm on time.

Stadt doesn't bother with a good morning but centers his one good eye on me and snaps, "I got oats for my stock, but should you dip into them for that nag it'll cost you a half dollar a day."

I don't honor that with a reply, so he reiterates. "A half dollar a day."

"We going where there's no graze?" I ask, my tone even.

"Don't plan to," he says.

"Then I don't plan to dip into your oats."

"Fine, tie that nag off to the wagon or let him run free. No matter to me."

I do tie him to the lead wagon, loosen his cinch and go forward to join Stadt where he's taken the driver's position and already has reins in hand. I remove my haversack and throw it into the lead wagon. I'll let Sandy carry his saddle with just enough cinch to keep it in place, and my own muzzle-loading rifle and shotgun in their saddle scabbards, just in case I have the need to mount quickly and be prepared for whatever comes.

"Shotgun is behind the seat," Stadt says. "You're to have it in hand sunup to lamps out, and near at hand all the night through. You'll be taking the last watch of the night from three AM to breakfast. First light is the time the savage will choose to attack, should we be cursed with trouble. I want young eyes and ears on duty at that prime time. That suit you?"

I can't help but smile. "Does is matter if it suits me?"

"Observant of you, Mister Zane," he says, then turns, gives a yell, "Wagons ho," and whips up the team.

We haven't made ten paces when I've decided that these two or three months might drag on like two or three years.

But the money's good, and we need it.

2

It's a long climb up and out of the Snake River canyon, and as we near the end of the day, I'm only three miles or so east of my own homestead. I'm tempted to ride over and say a second goodbye to my family and friends, but don't want to rile Stadt. It seems the hard man riles easy. That eye of his that's been scarred and gone milk-white gives me the wiggles and makes me look away when he glares at me. Pa would have chastised me and said look the man in the eye, even if the eye is ugly as a toad's belly.

I know this country and the folks who've made their home here for longer than any of us can judge and know them to be friends. Savages, as Stadt refers to the locals, the Nez Perce, is not my opinion, but his. Still, I'm compelled to rise at 3:00 a.m. and take the guard, letting Jasper Willoby, another guard and our hunter, catch a couple of hours of sleep.

Our crew consists of six men: Jasper, who's a mounted guard, hunter, occasional freighter, and longtime mountain man and trapper; Alabama, a black-bearded, slovenly fellow with a prodigious belly who calls himself Alabama and says that's his only name—which means to me he's likely on the run from the law—claims to be an expert packer and mule skinner; Maxwell Tennison who's tall as Stadt with light hair and beard, a pleasant smile, ice blue eyes, and an English accent, is the only one among us with tailored duds, refined speech and manners. Tennison carries a weapon to be admired, a 52 Sharps in .52 caliber with a strip of primers and new breech-loading paper cartridges. He carries paper and powder for constructing his own. He tells me the fine rifle cost him the proud sum of thirty dollars and is one of only one thousand six hundred built way back in Pennsylvania. The last man in our crew is Chang, a celestial who's both freighter, seamstress, harness maker and cook, and who sports a queue that hangs in a single braid to his waist. I soon learn Chang's English is limited and curses often in a rant of Chinee words I don't understand. But a curse is pretty dang obvious no matter the language. All wear sidearms. Chang carries a hatchet that he's never far from and is normally in a soiled red sash, pants with generous leg room, and sandals. I've watched him pull up his mount or the second wagon he sometimes reins, leap and scamper to some herb or greenery to harvest and bag it. I believe there's something to learn from all of them.

The good news is, even though Chang seems a serious fellow, I admire his biscuits and beef stew—he'd give my Ma and sis a run for the money with spatula and spoon. I immediately am pleased we won't go hungry so long as Chang has something in the larder. And Chang's as clean and kept as Alabama is slovenly and rough.

I soon learn from Jasper, that Maxwell Tennison is indeed an Englishman, hired by a Lord Willard Stanley-Smyth, who, for some reason I can't fathom, wants his goods to go overland from Coeur d'Alene to San Francisco. Jasper has surmised that Tennison was hired to make sure Stadt doesn't abscond with the Lord's possessions. I guess Lord Stanley-Smyth doesn't trust the steam-driven side-wheelers that I'm told ply the coast from Alaska to Mexico, and have since 1836, the year after I was born. I guess I understand, as many have gone to the bottom in Pacific storms and from boiler explosions.

We haven't gone three miles when Stadt hands the reins to me, stretches wide and yawns. "I'm climbing in the back for a little snooze. You can drive a team?"

"Six oxen from Missouri to here, when not driving our two mules pulling a cart."

"Right-wheel mule spooks with every sparrow takes flight, but other than that knot head they're real steady."

"I'm to drive with one hand?"

"What are you talking about?"

"You said I was to keep the shotgun in hand at all times."

"You are a smart ass are you not?"

"Repeating your words, Mister Stadt."

"Near at hand will do. Road ahead pulls up out of the canyon. Near five miles to gain the two thousand feet, I'm told. Ain't no rush, so pull up every five hundred feet of elevation, every hour or so, and let them blow. We got a long way to go.

He climbs over, retreats all the way to the back of the sixteen-foot wagon and reclines on those grain sacks of which he seems so proud.

We haven't gone a quarter mile until he's snoring like a riverboat steam engine, roaring and sputtering, and, in another quarter mile, one of the saddle backers pulls up alongside. He gives me a nod, stretches out a hand, and we shake.

"Jasper Willoby," he says, through a handlebar mustache as thick as his thumb.

And I answer, "Jake Zane."

He cranes his neck a little to see where Stadt is, then comes with a low laugh. "Signed you on as a shotgun guard, did he?"

I nod. He's captured my curiosity.

"He'll have you doing your work and his too. Keep you up twenty-four hours a day if he's able."

"Well, I know how to work, so long as I get a little sleep."

"He worked old Willy Simmons 'til he damn nigh went total looney, and that was just from Coeur d'Alene to here. I bet Willy didn't get ten hours sleep in five days. No wonder he slipped off the edge. In his head bone, I mean."

"Looney?"

"He was hired on as a shotgun guard too," Jasper again cocks an ear to make sure Stadt is snoring, then continues. "Willy started chewing Stadt out for trying to work him to death, shaking a fist at him and all. Stadt just drew that little '49' pocket Colt he carries and blew three .31 caliber holes in Jasper's brisket before you could say lickety-split. One of them while Willy was flat on his back in the dirt."

I stare at skinny Jasper a moment, then ask, "Did this Willy pull on him?"

"Willy always wore a hunting knife. He may have had a hand on the hilt, but it was sheathed."

"So, cold blood."

"Cold as a well digger's butt when up to his waist in ice water, if you ask me."

"That's the William fella buried in the Lewiston cemetery?"

"One and the same."

Stadt sputters in the back. Jasper gives me a little salute and reins away.

Our first three days and nights are uneventful, and I'm about to decide this the easiest money I'll ever come by.

We're camped on a rolling plain on the east edge of a place called Grand Ronde by Jasper, who claims to have trapped the huge valley where he dodged many Indians who took umbrage at his presence. He's brought in a fat doe, so we've enjoyed venison steak and red beans while he entertains us with tales of trapping and fighting shy of savages. Then he turns serious.

"These here parts is likely Yakima redskins. Soon we'll see the Blue Mountains to the west and in a week or so we'll cross them and be out of the Snake drainage—likely having to shed the wagons and go by mule train. The hell of it is, that's Wascupam, Cayuse, and Klamath redskin country. Them fellas ain't seen much of the white man and likely ain't got much respect for our long guns. They might trade and leave us be to pass peacefully. Then there be the Bannocks and beyond them the Paiutes as we near Californey. They've run hard against the white man and will likely want to skin us to cover their wickiups soon as they see us. They're sweethearts compared to the Modoc in Northern California. With luck, the California Guard will be running the Modoc hard and they'll be too busy to mess with us, but don't be counting on it." Then he lights the carved pipe he carries, takes a deep pull and turns to me.

Jasper narrows watery eyes, and asks, "Younger, you ever come face to face with a red man who wants your hair for his coup stick?"

"A few. I faced them down and found the white man more trouble than the red."

He laughs. "Well, boy, from your lips to God's ears.

I imagine you'll change your tune afore we reach Yerba Buena—I mean now San Francisco."

Stadt stands, scrapes his tin plate, and snaps at Jasper. "Don't be worryin' the men, Willoby. We got enough fire power to take on four dozen savages."

"That could be, Stadt. However, you might remember it was not long ago they hanged five Cayuse over in Oregon City for the Whitman massacre. Them folks was doing nothing but caring for them filthy Cayuses, and what they got for their trouble was being hacked to pieces. I can tell tales all night long about them tribes up ahead of us. Stay alert."

I can see Stadt getting red in the face and I'm wondering if steam ain't about to burst from his ears. He puts hands on hips. "Willoby, when I say don't worry the men, I expect you to shut that hole under your ugly nose. You do your job and let me worry about the savage."

Jasper gets to his feet and I'm wondering if he's about to get nose to nose with Stadt, but instead he heads for a nearby trickle of a stream, I guess to scrape and scrub his plate with sand.

"Hey," Stadt yells at him. Jasper stops. Stadt takes a step and hands him his tin plate. "Long as you're goin' that way, take care of this one."

Jasper eyes him for a moment, and I can see his jaw knot, but he reaches out, grabs the plate and strides off.

Alabama and Maxwell Tennison have chewed away, with eyes shifting from Jasper to Stadt and back as they trade words. They, too, rise and head for the stream, and I follow.

Jasper is finished and headed back to hand his plate to Chang. Stadt is mounting the lead wagon as he sleeps on the grain sacks under cover, so both are out of earshot.

As we scrub our plates, Tennison gives me a smile and

comments, "Any group of men have to vie for position. Seems Jasper has far more experience with this country than does Stadt, but Stadt is the boss man. It will all settle down soon enough."

"I ain't worried," I say, but it's a little bit of an exaggeration. If there truly are tribes of Indians who are savage ahead of us, I'd guess it would serve us well to be well led. I know one thing, ego has gotten many a man killed, and some of them died without their hair.

I guess it's prosaic that midmorning we see our first band of Indians. Two dozen—two of them with deer draped over the rumps of their paint horses—are lined up along a rise off to the east. The deer are a good sign. Savages fighting to gain provisions, to stay alive, can be downright fearful.

From this distance I can't tell if they're painted for war. That would be a bad sign, even if well fed.

3

"Just keep ploddin' along," Stadt orders. He's driving the lead wagon with me at his side nervously fingering the double barrel.

I ask, "You think I should mount up?"

"Sit where you are. Your first job is to protect your boss. Remember I'm the one reaches into my purse to pay you."

"Yes, sir, I just thought…"

"I'll do the thinkin' in this company." Then he turns and yells to Jasper. "You want to ride out and parley with them?" It's half question and half order.

Jasper reins up beside Stadt. "I'm a little surprised as them appear to be Shoshone or Snakes from over east. The hunting must be bad over their way or they wouldn't be here."

"Are they trouble?" Stadt asks.

"They ain't preachers or priests. Of course, they're by-God trouble. Let's just move along. I'd guess we're to go to the mules sometime tomorrow as there ain't no country to suit wagons over them Blue Mountains. We'll stand out less come then."

Stadt whips up the mules to a brisker walk. "We'll chop that row of stumps when we come to it."

Before he finishes his comment, we see two Indians break away from the others and head our way. At an easy canter.

Jasper sighs deeply, pulls his long gun, rests it across his thighs then turns to Stadt. "I guess parley is in order. Y'all might pull up next to that little copse of cottonwood up ahead. Them fat trunks will give you cover should things go sour. Hand me one of them axe heads you got for trading."

"Get one," Stadt says to me. I climb over the seat and fetch one, return and hand it to Stadt who passes it to Jasper.

"What are you gonna get in return?" Stadt snaps.

"I'm gonna get to keep my hair and you yours, God willing and the creek don't rise."

Stadt harrumphs showing some disgust as Jasper reins away and plods toward the two red men.

"You don't think that a good trade?" I ask Stadt, a tinge of disgust in my tone.

"Watch your mouth, Zane," he says, but doesn't take his eyes off Jasper, who's gigged his sorrel into a trot heading for the red men who've reined up halfway down the hill, halfway to us.

After another twenty-five yards we're threading our way into a stand of cottonwood. Stadt pulls up and dismounts the wagon. He waves Tennison, Alabama and Chang up to us. We all dismount, begin pulling downfall together and building ramparts of a sorry sort while Jasper, over a hundred yards east of us, reins up and begins talking, mostly in sign language, with the two tribesmen.

It's only moments when he sails the axe head out between them, and dust puffs up where the heavy head lands. Then he spins his sorrel and canters back our way. One of the Indians dismounts and retrieves the axe head.

Jasper ties his animal to a river willow and strides over.

"I think we'll pass without trouble," he says.

"You think?" Stadt snarls.

"Yep, I think. They about half understand me, and I about half understand them. They got meat so no need to steal our provisions and now they got a fine axe head. Like I said, I think we're fine. They did glance at our mules in a lascivious way."

"You're gettin' paid to know, not just think."

Jasper laughs sardonically. "They ain't no knowing when it comes to parleying with the savage. Next bunch we come to you're sure welcome to try your hand."

"Get back to ridin' drag. I don't want them sneakin' up on us."

Jasper gives him a little salute and, smiling as if happy with himself, reins away.

"That som'bitch will come to a bad end," Stadt says, somewhat under his breath.

"Then you'll have to parley. You know that sign language?" I ask.

He eyes me and furrows his brow as he snarls, "And you're likely to be right on his tail."

"Mister Stadt, all I want to do is my job and get paid as agreed."

"Then do it with a shut pie hole."

"Suits me," I say.

He's quiet for a moment, then adds, "One of these days, you thinkin' you have to have the last word, will get your head busted."

I decide this might be a good time not to reply, so I don't.

***

The next morning, one hour into the day, we find ourselves facing a ravine that's cut a hundred feet deep by a fairly fast-moving but narrow stream, running east out of the now much closer Blue Mountains. We can see the stream emerges from a steep walled canyon in the Blues. Jasper scouts to the east while we twiddle our thumbs and wait. In only a half hour he returns, shaking his head.

"This is it. This trickle dumps into what I figure must be the Owyhee River, and that cut is well over two hundred feet deep down near the bigger flow. Lessen y'all want to spend a couple of month's road building, we're gonna train up the mules from here on."

"Ride on upstream," Stadt snaps. "See if there's a good place to hide the wagons. Never know, I might want to recover them someday."

Jasper takes off to the west while we dismount in a small copse of cottonwood and begin unloading our two wagons. For the first time I grasp the weight of our cargo—well wrapped packages about the size of a small loaf of bread weighing like lead. I'd guess fifteen pounds to the package. Jasper has told me we're carrying treasure from the mines and panning between Coeur d'Alene and the crowns of the Selway Mountains, and now I believe him. I'm a bit bamboozled as we've heard of no strikes or gold rush to the area. Whoever found this bounty has kept mum. No wonder Stadt, or maybe I should say Lord Stanley-Smyth, is willing to pay a hundred-dollar bonus should the freight arrive safely. If gold is bringing sixteen dollars the ounce…damned if I don't need a pencil to cypher what each loaf must be worth. Sixteen ounces times sixteen dollars times fifteen, whatever that is. I know one thing. It's a hell of a lot. And that's just for one of the many loaves of 'bullet lead'.

Tennison sees me straining, and says, "Damn bullet lead is heavy."

"So's gold."

He gives me a knowing smile. "Silver too."

I laugh. We must have unloaded three, maybe four, hundred pounds of 'bullet lead', as well as our stores and tools. Before we break for lunch. I'm thinking as we dine on beans and side meat, and flat bread that Chang makes light as fluffed cotton, that sixteen ounces to the pound and sixteen dollars to the ounce times all these pounds, is so dang much money, if truly gold, I can't figure it without a slate and chalk. It's so much Mr. Stadt's company can afford to abandon two four-hundred-dollar wagons and valuable harness without a qualm.

Jasper returns and reports, "We got to knock down a few small cottonwoods, but dang if there ain't a fine cave in that cliff yonder that will hold these wagons with space to spare. It'll take us a day to get them there, but they'll be outta the weather. There's a trickle of water coming outta the cave, but not enough to worry things."

"Then let's get to swingin' axes," Stadt yells, then snaps at Chang who's repacking his cooking implements into paniers. "You, too, Chang. Grab an axe and work up a few blisters."

It's a hard day using muscles that haven't been axe-tested for some time. We fell two evergreens so they cover the cave entrance, leaving one still partially attached to its stump, hoping it will remain green. Then Jasper, Alabama, Tennison and I climb the slope above the opening and roll all the stones we can to partially block the opening, but only stones small enough for a man, maybe two, to heave aside. We not only get the wagons fifty feet deep into the mountain, but get the tracks leading there eradicated; swept away with pine boughs. There's nothing we can do about an obvious wagon-wide road through the copse of young cottonwood, and stumps cut only a foot above the soil, so we chop a few trees to each side so it's not so obvious and drop them into the roadway.

It's the best we can do.

I saw my share of savages on the way west on the Oregon Trail, but there was something about the bunch we just passed that caused me to sleep restless. If I woke once, I woke a dozen times. And I'm awake when Tennison comes to toe me and tell me it's my go at guarding. He advised me he's stirred the coals under the coffee pot.

A steaming cup of muddy coffee in hand, I take my place standing watch at 3:00 a.m. I'm not surprised at the loud snoring coming from the men in camp. It's all I can do to stay awake after eight hours of swinging an axe and only five hours of shuteye, but it's good I do, otherwise I wouldn't have heard the distant neigh of a horse then a nicker from another in return. As my head was nodding, I'd shed my coat using the cold of night to help keep me awake. And thank the good Lord I'm not sawing logs. Particularly since Stadt announced he'd horsewhip any man found sleeping on guard duty and hang him should it happen a second time. I quickly count the animals on our picket line, at first thinking one or two might have wandered off, then I snap to full awake, with a chill down my backbone, as I realize they're all there.

So, who's out there in the diminishing darkness. There's a thin line of light to the east turning the black sky to a blue wash all along the horizon.

If Indians only attack at dawn, I figure I've got about fifteen minutes to see who's come to call on our camp.

I hurry from bedroll to bedroll giving each a kick or prod with the butt of my rifle and a fast whisper.

"We got company," I say to each, and each man springs to life. Before the sun tops the low mountains to the east, our six men surround the camp, all facing out, half of them in long Johns and boots, but armed and ready.

And we wait.

4

If they're out there, they're real good at putting the sneak on—except for that telltale whinny of two mustangs. The trickle we've camped by is lined with willows, and some blue sage spots the rising meadow beyond the dozen cottonwoods we've camped among. At our back is some thick chokecherry that would hide a herd of buffalo could they remain quiet. And the savage has proven to me, many a time, he can be silent as a creeping fog and just as chilling.

I'm hunkered down behind a pannier with my cap and ball rifle in hand, my own scattergun near at hand, the double barrel Mr. Stadt has assigned me beside it, and my Colt holstered on my hip. I figure, should I catch a target at a distance, I'll let fly with the .50 cal, then I have four loads of heavy buckshot in the two doubles and six in the Colt's spinner. The twelve mules, six horses plus my Sandy are on a pair of picket lines between two cottonwoods, nearer the stream.

Tennison, with his Sharps, stands atop a blowdown cottonwood more than three feet in diameter, leaning against the trunk of a smaller one. That gives him some elevation but also makes a fine target of him if they come out of the chokecherry behind us. Jasper is to my left a few paces, Alabama to my right, both hunkered down behind panniers as am I. Mr. Stadt has taken a position in one of the now empty wagons, just his eyes and floppy brimmed hat showing above the sideboards. Chang is at his side, with a hatchet in one hand and his meat cleaver in the other.

Without being instructed, all of us remain as silent as a slimy slug under a rock.

Until Alabama mutters just loud enough for all of us to hear. "They be out there. I can smell 0'em."

I have to shake my head and feel a half-smile, which surprises me a little as smiling while presuming you're in the sights of a savage with arrow nocked seems a bit out of sorts. Alabama is a foul man and how he could smell a skunk over his own whiffiness stumps me, but maybe he can.

Just as the sun peeks over the horizon, and rays penetrate the black sky, they break from all around us, screaming like eagles mating. Tennison is the first to find a target and the 1852 slant-breech Sharps kicks in his hands.

"One down," he yells as he breaks the breech and feeds in another paper cartridge.

Alabama and I both find a target. The Indian's arms fly up and his bow spins off into the underbrush. I don't know which of us, maybe both, hit the man, but at less than fifty paces I'd be surprised if I missed as he was running straight at me.

I don't bother to try and reload my muzzle loader but rather pick up my scattergun and cock both barrels. My trigger finger finds the forward trigger as I search for movement. An arrow creases the top of my shoulder and I inadvertently fire the left barrel, uselessly into the sage.

That's a reflex I'll have to watch.

I cuss myself, but the arrow passed on by—it's not protruding from my flesh—so I don't take the time to check the wound. I find the second trigger just as a savage with a wicked stone axe in hand—his face striped in black and yellow, a fur hat of skunk hide, wearing nothing more than breech cloth and moccasins wrapped calf high—breaks out of the sage at only twenty paces away.

I swing on him and pull when he's less than fifteen and misfire as nothing happens. I can feel my stomach tighten but feel hollow as a gourd, and my jaw clamps.

Luckily, with a roar to my left, he spins away and his thrown battle axe soars over my head.

I see that Jasper has come to my aid, then realize a savage is nearly upon him as he's fighting to free his sidearm.

I repay the favor with the right barrel, which fires. I spin to retrieve my second scattergun as an arrow slams into the pannier, and another buzzes close nearly parting my hair.

We fire another half-dozen rounds then all goes quiet.

All of us take the opportunity to reload as gun smoke sears our nostrils as it drifts away.

"That be it," Jasper calls out.

"Sounds so," Alabama answers.

"Hold on," Tennison says from his high perch. I see him seeming to judge distance, then very carefully adjust the rear sight on the Sharps. He seems to take a breath, hold it, and fires.

"Another to my credit, gentlemen," he says and dismounts from the cottonwood blowdown. "Near three hundred yards, I'd surmise," he says and flashes a smile.

The sun is only half over the horizon, and it seems the battle is over.

Only then do I realize my shoulder is nicely creased

and blood is causing my shirt to stick to my chest.

Tennison strides over, eyes my shoulder and yells at Chang, who's now standing in the bed of the wagon. Stadt has still not risen from his hiding place, and I wonder if he fired a shot during the short but fairly ferocious battle.

"What the hell?" Tennison exclaims.

I've been trying to remove my shirt as Chang is digging into a satchel as he comes my way. I presume to dress the little groove on my shoulder, but I turn to see both Jasper and Alabama hard at work scalping the first of three Indians I see spread-eagle on the ground. One suddenly moves, rolling back and forth, badly wounded, but not crying out. Alabama, I guess not wanting to waste a load, palms a rock bigger than his fist, strides over and bashes the Indian two or three times until he stills.

"What, exactly, are you doing?" Tennison snaps at Jasper who's continuing his work peeling the Indian's scalp away.

"Most of 'em don't think they can fly away to heaven should they not have their topknot. They'll think twice about coming at us, they know we know their ways," Jasper says, without stopping his work or looking up.

Alabama is performing the same savage act on the other Indian.

Tennison shakes his head, then turns and strides over to the wagon. "You decide to take a nap in there, Stadt," he says with a grin that looks as much smirk as amusement.

"I do my share, my dandy friend," Stadt says as he stands in the back of the wagon and brushes off his trousers, then he turns to Chang, "Are you gonna get us some grub or be a sogger?"

"No sogger. Cook." Chang says and leaps from the wagon. His iron works are already in place, and he has a stack of wood left over from supper, so he's soon hard at it.

"Fetch a mule at a time," he yells at me. "Let's divvy this load up among the mules and get saddled up. I want to make twenty miles today."

I'm soon proving my worth as a packer by throwing diamond hitches to secure pannier-covering tarps on the mules. But as I work, I'm wondering about Stadt, who's standing aside sipping Chang's coffee as the rest of us load up. Being the boss and not pitching in is one thing, but I don't think he showed more than his eyes over the sideboards of the wagon when the lead was buzzing the camp and never fired a shot.

It won't do to be working for a man with a yellow streak.

If this morning was any example, we'll need all six guns at work should trouble come again. And it damn sure will.

At the least, I've acquired a couple of fine souvenirs. A scar from an Indian arrow that was four inches from sending me to my knees before Saint Peter begging to enter the pearly gates, and a fine stone-head war club adorned with bead work and eagle feathers.

At Jasper's insistence, we leave the bodies to the scavengers, or to be recovered by their tribe. An example, he says. I wonder. Could such disrespect merely anger the enemy? A jab in the eye of a far superior enemy, at least in numbers.

I guess it's something to ponder as we ride into tight treed and brush-lined canyons where a man, or other danger, could be three strides from you and unseen.

5

Stadt lined us out for the continued trip.

Far in the lead, at least two hundred yards, Jasper plods along picking our trail and scouting for water, campsites, and danger.

Chang is next, leading two mules packed with his cooking implements and larder.

I'm number three, leading a pack string of four mules.

Stadt follows, sandwiched, I figure, between as many guns as possible.

Alabama follows, also leading a string of four.

The remaining two horses follow Alabama, running free, but seeming to have no interest in leaving their chums.

Tennison rides drag, leading a pair of mules.

In that train configuration, we start up into the Blue Mountains. I soon note much higher mountains to the west, so it seems we are merely in the foothills of the Blues.

Strung out as we are, each with a string, other than Stadt, doesn't make for much socializing. After four hours, we break aside a trickle to rest the horses and lunch on jerky, hardtack, and water. As seems his habit, Chang moves up and down the trickle picking watercress and wild onions.

Jasper seems to have taken a shine to me and sidles over to jaw.

"I done studied our backtrail when we topped that wee pass a ways back. Seems we discouraged them filthy redskins."

I study him for a moment as I chew my jerky, then ask, "I had friends among the Nez Perce who had a seasonal village only two miles from my homestead. I didn't find them to be filthy."

"Oh, they be clean enough. That ain't what makes 'em filthy to my way of thinking."

"Then what does?" I ask.

"Did you never see the leavin's after they raided a wagon train or outpost."

"Can't say as I have," I answer, gnawing off another bite.

"Then you got a sight to see, younger. After the men have their way with any captives, usually killing those they judge brave right off, but maybe killing any others slow-like, the women have at the corpses. They'll chop and saw until the dead is spread all over hell and gone, and maybe even cut your manhood off and stuff it in your mouth, or in the mouth of one of the other luckless louts what gave up the ghost."

"I have heard some of that, and if their actions is what you mean by filthy, then I agree." None of this was a subject I wanted to dwell upon, so I changed the subject. "Will we come upon any settlements before we reach California?"

"A handful of days, likely not more than three, we'll come upon Brownsville. In the Grande Ronde."

I shrug. "Grande Ronde?"

"A beautiful valley. Had y'all not headed north along the Snake you'd a followed the main trail into the Grande Ronde Valley. A fella named Brown settled there and has a trading post and small mill. Fine folks. Nursed me after I took a Paiute arrow in my buttock. Them ladies peeled me down like an onion or like they was skinning a boar hog and dug that arrowhead outta me. Had I not been red-faced with fever, I'd a been red-faced with them seeing all God gave me."

I had to laugh at that. But then got serious again. "We gonna have to face down the savage again?"

"Maybe. More likely after we head southwest outta the Grande Ronde. The good of that country is the savage may never have seen a white man. The bad? The savage may never have seen a white man."

Jasper laughed and slapped his thighs. Then he added, "They'll likely have a good old highfalutin' time skinning a critter white as you."

I notice he has one of the scalps hanging from the muzzle of his cap and ball rifle. "Dang, Jasper, I'd think they'd wanna start on you, being as how you seem to be crowing about skinning one of their own."

"Let's move it," Stadt yelled, and we pulled the picket pins of our particular mules from where we'd staked them along the trickle to water and graze. In less than fifteen minutes, we're again eating the dust of those ahead.

After another four hours on a trail not much more than game-made, Jasper returned from scouting ahead.

I overheard him palavering with Stadt.

"Another three miles over near rise and there be a fine meadow, belly deep with grass, flanking a deep, slow-moving stream. Grasshoppers is busy and trout is breaking the surface. I've a mind for some fresh fish. Suit you?"

"It does. Go on ahead and wet a line while we catch up."

"You got a steep trail around the mountain and dropping down to the meadow, so take it slow."

"How steep?"

"Steep, but doable. It's that'a'way or backtracking three or four miles and taking our chances on another route."

"I don't want no train wrecks. You best not be leading us into harm's way. Maybe you oughta take the boy's string and let him do the easy task."

To my pleasure, Jasper laughed. "Hell, pilgrim, that boy's a hand. The rest of y'all should be as good with a team or a string."

"Then go on and catch us a mess. Earn your keep."

Jasper shook his head, not fond of being doubted, but gave him a nod, spun his mount and moved on ahead at a brisk walk.

The country was becoming rougher, from rolling pine, chokecherries, willow lined creeks, and ravines, to sharp shouldered lichen-spotted granite cliffs, with scraggly cedars and buck brush jutting from clefts. Wide game trails became narrow ledges with occasional steep drop offs.

Where water creeped across the ledge, it challenged mule and horse to keep their footing.

At one point, we moved beneath a two-foot-wide spray that was a forty-foot waterfall splattering on the rocks below, dividing into a dozen rivulets before they married again below the rampart.

The surefooted mules seemed hardly distracted by the danger, but the horses neighed and whinnied, and occasionally when I glanced back, I could see their nostrils flare and eyes widen. Seeing white all around those large brown pupils made me tighten thighs against the saddle.

Then when upon a dangerous spot, I changed tactics and posted in the saddle, sitting loose with only toes in the stirrups. If Sandy made a misstep, I wanted to quickly unload, both for my sake and Sandy's.

On the inside turns of the narrow trail, the ravines, the fall was ofttimes only a gentle slope. Then on the outside turns, the ridges, the fall was occasionally a hundred feet or more.

It was on an outside turn when I spotted Jasper two or three hundred feet below and nearly a quarter mile away next to a slow meandering river, jumping up and down and waving his arms like a mad man.

Jasper is not easily excited.

I quickly surveyed the slope above, then turned and looked behind. The horses seemed particularly upset. I learned long ago that my dog and horse, or any other four-legged or winged critter nearby, have far better senses than do I. If they have ears forward, snorting, growling, or flying to a treetop, it's time to be on guard. Nearly fifty yards ahead, Chang is now in the lead as Jasper has ridden ahead to catch us a mess of trout. Chang's horse is single footing nervously, and before he reaches the outside of the steep ridge, the mules sit back, jerk away, and scramble with forefeet up the steep slope to spin on hind legs and reverse direction. Both do as Chang yells back over his shoulder as his charges charge back the way they'd come.

There is no room for them to pass Sandy and me and my four mules, but they're coming at a gallop. I thought I'd secured those loads as tight as my pa's saddle tree joints, but gear is flying everywhere as they buck, hump, jump, and scrape up against the rock wall.

Then I see Chang's mount go crazy, bucking stiff-legged, trying to shed himself of his load—and he does. Chang does a half-somersault, landing on his back on the narrow trail, then slips off and tumbles to a ledge ten feet below, his body wedged between two rocks.

And it's probably a good thing he's slung off the trail, as a yearling grizzly comes into view. As it perches on the trailside looking down at the yelling man, another rounds behind it and pauses to look down.

Then I'm not surprised to see mama grizzly, two and a half times the size of the yearlings, as she pads up to join them.

She eyes the man below, snorts, but he is too far to take a swipe at so the eight-hundred-pound gray grizzly with a black hump barks a slathering snap at her cubs. They oblige by trotting on our way. Chang is lucky, even I know bears are at a disadvantage if you're downhill... front legs are slightly shorter than back.

So, she's coming on my way.

And there is nowhere to go.

6

I slip the scattergun from its scabbard. Even my faithful Sand Bay is beginning to shiver and back into the mule behind, so I slip off uphill and am able to lie against the rock wall. I threw the lead rope to my mule string, but the four behind me are strung together. As the lead yearling nears, they tangle on the trail.

Scrambling down, I'm back in the flat of the trail, with the lead bear now only twenty-five paces and still coming, not at a run but a curious slow lope.

Glancing over my shoulder hearing a squeal, I see the four mules plunging off the ledge. They scream as they tumble in a mess of lead rope, scattering packs and tarps, and flailing legs.

The good news is they've left the trail open a good ways for Sandy, who's leaving me to my own device, escaping at a gallop.

I have both barrels of the twelve-gauge cocked, but as the two smaller bears are ahead of mama and are my first challenge, I draw the Colt.

The lead yearling, a cinnamon, draws up no more than fifteen yards from me. He snorts as if he has some stink in his nose, then stands, his forelegs out at the ready like he was a waiter delivering a tray of treats.

I'm hoping against all hope that he'll drop to all four, spin and confront his brother and mama, and all will decide I'd be too tough or stinky to gnaw, but he doesn't. He drops back and cocks one foreleg like a hound pointing a sage grouse.

He backs a half step and I'm thinking I can breathe. Then his brother crowds him from the rear, placing both forepaws on his brother's butt and is half-upright looking over his brother's back.

I guess the cinnamon decides that brushing me off the trail is less trouble than turning around. With his first step my way, I let fly one into his shoulder. Then as he roars his displeasure, I fire another into his other shoulder. Had it been mama, I'm sure she'd have been on me before I could ratchet the hammer for the second shot, but cinnamon is unsure. I chose the shoulder shots, as I've been taught to break a bear down as they die hard and long.

He's up again on his hind legs, shedding his brother off his back, and my third shot takes him in the throat. He's still not down but rather spins and tangles with the second yearling who swats him, and he goes over the edge, tumbling ass over teakettle down the slope.

His brother is angry and charges me full tilt. I have the double hanging at my side and don't even get it to my shoulder but pull off from the waist. The eight .32 caliber balls are too much for the little hundred-pound bear, and he stands, slinging blood and slobber as he goes over backward into his mama who's trying to get to me. But there's been too many of her offspring in the way.

I drop to one knee, praying that the second barrel doesn't misfire. This time I have the scattergun on my shoulder as mama bear crawls right over the top of cinnamon. Were a full-grown bull buffalo charging me on that narrow trail, it wouldn't seem larger than this horrible tooth-gnashing monster.

The twelve-gauge kicks in my hands, but she merely shakes her head. I fling the scattergun and take an escape route I had hoped wouldn't be necessary. There's a cleft in the cliff on my right. With a few hand and foot holds, and with my Colt holstered and my shotgun flung away, I scramble up.

She's throwing her head back and forth slinging spittle and blood and moving forward. With a quick glance, I realize at least one of her eyes is shattered. I'm praying both are.

I think I'm going to clamber out of her reach. Then claws rip through my elk-hide trousers, and I'm sucked backward out of the cleft, hard, back-down to the ledge, and she's on me. I manage to get my hands over my eyes, then feel her weight crushing me against the rough stone ledge.

I hear a roar, then realize it's the second of the same sound, from behind me somewhere.

I can't breathe with the weight on my chest, then suddenly am gasping, sucking in deep lungfuls of cold fresh air. Tennison bends over me, I guess to see if I'm still alive. His Sharps is in hand, still smoking.

Tennison is joined by Alabama, both are standing over me. The huge bear has rolled off the ledge, I presume with their effort, and disappeared over the edge. Her cinnamon offspring is lying in the trail sucking wind but no longer in the fight, and the other yearling is disappearing around a distant bend in the trail.

I wipe the blood out of my eyes, not knowing if it's mine or bear blood, and see Tennison is reloading.

"Anything broke?" Alabama asks, and pats me down on chest and shoulders.

I manage to sit up. "How the…how the heck…would I know?" I ask. "I hurt…damn nigh…everywhere."

"That's a good'n," he says, and laughs. "If'n you hurt, you ain't dead."

"Anybody else injured," I manage to ask, and try to quell the shaking that's starting low and ascending my backbone.

"Chang is scratched and bruised. Hear him cuss?" he says, and I do. I don't understand a word but look over the edge to see Chang trying to put his kitchen wares back into a pannier. Another pannier is farther down the slope, and only one of the mules who went over is standing. The second is bawling with an obvious bent and broken leg and is wedged back down between some boulders.

"Stadt?" I ask, through shattering teeth. I wish I could blame it on the cold, but it's pure left-over fear. It's finally gotten to me. I didn't have time to quake while all that was happening.

"Horse threw him," Alabama says with a chuckle, "then he beat trail chasing his mount back toward Lewiston, and likely running from the fray. He might have a few blisters from beating feet."

Tennison helped me to my feet. "I got your animal tied to a bit of brush back down the trail a ways. If you don't have something broken that needs tending, we'd better get to seeing what we can save of our gear."

As he spoke, Stadt strode up behind him. "Anybody need buryin'?" he asked, in such a casual manner it caused heat to rise in my pained backbone. His nonchalance at the possibility of someone's demise angered me and at least cause my quivering to stop.

Tennison turned to him. "Not so's you'd notice."

"Then let's get to gatherin' up our goods and put the string back together if we can find them. Four pack mules passed me like I was tied to a post. No matter what else, we got to recover our cargo."

"At least two animals will need putting down," Tennison said.

As he spoke Jasper rode up. "Tried to warn y'all. Damn bears ran me into the creek, and I got my powder wet or I'd a fired a couple of warning shots. Everybody whole?"

Stadt didn't bother to answer his question, rather asked, "Did you catch a string of fish?"

"Had us a half dozen, average fifteen inches, but the damn bears et 'em."

"Then finish off them mules and we'll be roastin' mule backstrap. Right now, I gotta see to our cargo."

Jasper cackled a little, then added, "Ol' bear ain't bad on the plate and we damn sure got plenty of that."

Stadt lowered himself off the ledge and picked his way down, searching every nook and cranny between boulders in the escarpment below for the well wrapped, heavy loaves and whatever gear he could find. Then he yelled at me to help. I started over the edge, then realized I was hurt more than I figured. I bent, putting my hands on my knees and wheezed some which hurt so damn bad it was all I could do not to yell. Yelling would likely hurt worse.

Tennison yelled at Stadt, "The boy is gonna lie flat for a while. He's earned his day's wages already."

Stadt frowned up at him but said nothing as I found a flat spot to lie back, breathing as deeply as I could with what I figured were badly bruised, if not broken, ribs. Every breath said you just had a huge bear on your chest. If there was a choice, I wouldn't breathe. But there was no choice.

Jasper mounted up and headed back the way we'd come to run down the other mules and gather up goods from scattered packs.

My old pa used to say, "Tomorrow's another day." I dang sure hope it's better than this one.

7

At supper, with a too-large fire near the slow-moving river where Jasper was fishing when the bears came, Tennison, Alabama and Jasper ganged up on Stadt. Stadt was eager to pack up, splitting the load between all ten mules, but the others insisted we rest at least a day in this fine camp spot. Two of our mules were favoring a leg, one with his hock tore open with a sharp rock shard I'd guess; the second was merely gimpy. One of our horses had disappeared and not shown back up. So, we had no spare horse should one go lame, and only our pack mules.

Tennison blamed his wanting to lay over on the lame mules, but I suspected he was worried about my innards and the fact I was having trouble catching my breath. Most every half hour, he checked on me, brought me cold water from the river and hot broth he'd insisted Chang make. I would laugh if it didn't hurt so damn much but smiled when I thought of broth from the meat of the two dead bears helping to cure me. I guess that's justice.

Even with a full day's rest, I had to gasp and my eyes watered with the pain when, the following morning, I swung up into the saddle. However, I presumed my ribs were only bruised, not busted. Thanks be to the good Lord, the country eased, with no more rock ledges or narrow places with hundred-foot drops.

On the morning of the third day after tangling with the grizzlies, we topped a pine and what Jasper taught me was Oregon White Oak covered mountain and looked down on what Jasper said was Grand Ronde. Far below I made out a tendril of smoke.

"Civilization?" I yelled up to where Jasper had reined up to wait for us.

"Such as it is. Last I was here they was a trading post, mill, saloon, three or four log cabins and, a ways down the trail, a bawdy house. You ever been to a bawdy house, boy?"

I shrugged. "Not only never been but can only guess what it might be."

"Why, tarnation, boy. You some kinda bluenose or what? Pure pleasure, younger. Pure pleasure in a pleasure parlor." He guffawed again.

"Where do they get their customers way out here?" I figured four cabins couldn't support even a handful of soiled doves.

Jasper laughed hard as he reined up beside me and reached for my lead rope. I'd been having to turn half around once in a while, my arm stretched back, when my four pack mules failed to keep up. It pained my back and ribs something awful when I did. I'd tried to tie my lead rope off to my saddle horn, but it's a dangerous way to lead—risking mules sitting back and jerking your horse off his feet. The lead rope constantly cuts across your thigh. I didn't need another injury.

I gladly handed him the lead. "Thank you, Mister Jasper," I said, and dang sure meant it.

It took us over an hour to reach the valley floor, and

we came into the little village—now, I noted, with a church—if that was the meaning of a steeple and bell—at the same time a wagon train of over four dozen prairie schooners circled in a nearby meadow.

"Maybe a hoedown tonight," Alabama yelled as we spied the wagons in the distance.

"And a bevy of split tails?" Jasper said, slapping his thighs as he laughed.

Alabama was nearest me, so I asked, "Split tails. That some kind of bird?"

That made Alabama laugh even louder than Jasper had. Then he said, "Women, boy, the fair sex. Them what took a bite outta the apple and we all been paying since."

I merely shrugged again. Brown had forty acres of meadow with a trickle of a creek fed by a spring flowing a spurt the size of your thumb. The wagon train turned out their oxen, horses, mules and a few sheep and goats there. We were assigned a half acre behind the trading post for our mules and horses. It was next to a small log barn—yet to be caulked—with a livery sign over its double doors.

Tennison helped us corral the animals, after we'd dumped their packs, while Stadt stored the packs and our gear in the building marked "livery".

Chang provisioned in the trading post—we'd been unable to find our coffee, sugar, and our last pork belly after the crash. He made the post just before they closed and then fixed us a fine meal of buttermilk fresh from the post's churn, biscuits slathered in butter and honey, bacon, beans, and the season's first picking of mustard greens cooked in bacon grease and vinegar, all topped off with a pie made from dried cherries, apples and molasses.

Then all of us headed for the circle of wagons, with banjo and fiddle music already ringing across the meadow, and what Alabama called a bevy of split tails.

Jasper and Alabama pitched in and bought a gallon jug of corn liquor from Mrs. Brown, who was said to distill the finest this side of Kentucky. They led with it as we threaded our way through wagon tongues into the double circle.

It was a good ploy as we and the jug were damn sure welcomed.

There was not one but two banjos, a fiddle, and a pianoforte playing in the center. I had to admire folks who'd managed to get all the way to Oregon with a pianoforte, even if only a sixth the size of an upright piano. I plopped down on the meadow next to the musicians, hummed along as they played and enjoyed watching Alabama and Jasper kicking up their heels dancing jigs in circles among the couples. As the sun dropped behind the last of the Blue Mountains to the west, I noticed some of the younger, and a few of the older, male pilgrims slip away. Jasper and Alabama had been freely sharing the gallon jug of happy juice, and some of those fellas hadn't tasted liquor in weeks.

Slip away they did, in the direction of the bawdy house, which I knew to be a little more than half a mile to the west.

Jasper walked over and pulled me to my feet. "Done heared they got a couple of young ones down the way."

"Young ones?" I asked.

"Split tails, boy. Youngers, like yourself."

Before I could reply, Tennison stopped from dancing a whirl around us with a middle-aged lady in a gown as blue as a cornflower and hair like corn silk. He tipped his hat at her and hurried up behind Jasper.

"I'll bet I know what this old reprobate is up to," Tennison said, laying a hand on Jasper's shoulder.

"Reprobate?" Jasper looked a bit confounded. "What

the blue devil hell is a reprobate."

Tennison ignored him and turned to me. "Boy, you know what the pox is?"

"Yes, sir," I replied.

"Well, you can walk shy of getting it, and going crazy as a Saint Louis looney house full of bedbugs and lice."

"How so?" I asked, thinking I'd be happy to know that trick.

"Stay out of those bawdy houses, that's how."

"Hell's fire, Tennison," Jasper sputtered. "There's some ladies down there tender and pretty as Sunday mornin'. This boy needs to cut his teeth on somethin' tender."

"Don't do it boy, there's lot of nice young ladies on this train."

"I guess it won't hurt to see what's going on in one of these bawdy houses." I said.

Tennison merely shrugged as the little band struck up another tune, then walked away. "It's your life, boy," he said, waving over his shoulder.

"There's about a swig left," Jasper said, and held the jug out.

I took it, and wet my lips, but that was it. It was a taste I'd yet to acquire.

"We going?" I asked.

Jasper waved Alabama over. He handed the jug to the fellas in the band, accepted their thanks, and strode out, waving us along.

I caught up with Jasper, who glanced over and said, "Don't ya be worrying about old Tennison, he's a portmanteau."

"Sorry?" I said, having no idea what he'd said.

"He's a portmanteau, the king's man. He carries the shield of the Lord of the Manor, his eminence Lord Willard Stanley-Smyth, who's the stud duck of this outfit, even though he don't grace us with his presence."

"What's that got to do with me seeing the goings on in that bawdy house?"

"Not a dang thing, boy. Like the king's man said, it's your life. That's why we whomped all them redcoats four score ago. It damn sure is your life."

"Seems right to me," I said. "On to the bawdy house."

8

As the three of us strode up to the two-story log house, I could hear the raucous singing along with the plinking of a banjo and the stomping of feet, somewhat in time to the music. The place was well lit with more glass windows than I've seen since we left Missouri.

A rather buxom lady with carrot-colored hair, dressed in a bright green gown with what were once white buttonhook shoes that covered her ankles up as high as the hem of the long gown, leaned on the railing surrounding the porch. She was smoking a pipe, drawing and blowing smoke between laughing as if she'd never heard anything so funny before. Three fellas, who I'd seen earlier at the hoedown in the wagon circle, were jawing with her. She had a long bright-blue peacock feather stuck into the pile of hair on her head. Her cheeks and lips were reddened and eyelids colored green to match the gown. The dress was cut low enough that there was a canyon between those large examples of womanhood. Some apparatus must have been under that gown to make them bulge up like that. She had a daisy shoved into that cleft, the orange center of which matched the color of her hair and the freckles on her cheeks, and what was visible of her chest was spotted with same. All this on skin as white as a lizard's belly.

I'd never see the like of it, even when the occasional medicine wagon came to relieve us of our money on the Oregon Trail. A couple of those ladies, including a gypsy thought to be a witch, kept me wide-eyed at the costumes they wore, but none as fancy as this.

When we reached the stairs to the wide porch, she stepped away from the other three, coming our way.

"Why, howdy, gents. Welcome to Mandy Mays from Manistee, Michigan, who runs the best pleasure house this side of the mighty Mississippi. You'll be happy to know you are face to face with the mistress of the house, her very own self. I do hope you didn't come just to admire the wares as we hit the jackpot tonight, near full up, and ain't gonna tolerate merely eyeballing the goods."

Jasper laughed. "Why, ma'am, if'n you done hit the jackpot you won't be needin' my pocket fulla coin."

She slapped him on the shoulder, but friendly like, and said, "If them pockets are full to the brim, go on in. I got a couple of barrels of new beer and a keg of Missus Brown's fine whiskey. Only a dime for a mug of suds and a quarter dollar for three fingers of the dew of the corn. You should have a few dollops to gain courage while you're waiting in line for the ladies."

Then she turned her attention to me. "Why, if this isn't a picture of young manhood. The girls will be flipping a coin to gain your favor. I presume you've ridden a wild one before?"

"Ma'am…" I stuttered a little. "I've been throwed, but not in the last few years."

"Well, young fella, my girls won't throw you far, but you can't wear your spurs as they cut up my sheets."

"Ma'am," I mumbled.

"Ain't you the cutest one," she said. Then wrapped a hand around the back of my neck and jerked my nose between those big melons putting me eye to eye with those orange freckles while she wiggled herself back and forth. She laughed as she let me escape. "Ain't that the sweetest daisy you ever got a whiff of?"

All the men were laughing and slapping their thighs.

I couldn't answer, except for the fact I knew my face was as red as her lips and hot as a branding iron. Not only was I embarrassed about where my nose was pulled into, but my back and ribs hurt so I was surprised tears didn't streak my cheeks. I gasped and wheezed, not from embarrassment but from the pain, and the men laughed even louder.

I did not enjoy being the brunt of the humor.

Spinning on my heel I headed for the door. No matter how I hurt, I hadn't come this far not to see what went on inside. Jasper and Alabama, still chuckling, followed close on my heels.

I pushed through the door, which had four panes of glass and lace curtains, and had to take another deep breath as the walls were covered with some kind of fancy, red, patterned paper. The ceiling was fancy, patterned, hammered tin tiles in a repetition. There was a bar all along the west wall with at least two dozen stools covered in hair out of ox or cowhide. A brass spittoon was located near the brass foot rail, spaced every four stools. Also, between every four stools, hung a black towel under the bar. I guess to mop the foam out of patron's mustaches and beards.

The back bar held more bottles and kinds of hooch than I knew existed, except for a six-foot opening in the middle in which hung a five-foot-long by three-foot-high painting, oil paint I imagined, of a reclining, scantily-clad lady with one nipple exposed. I guess that wasn't the first time I'd gazed on a woman's bare breast as I'd been told I was nursed when a baby, but it's the first I can remember. They were very large breasts and it made me wonder if it wasn't a portrait of Miss Mandy Mays. If so, it was when she was much younger and thinner.

Six round tables with six captain's chairs each were spaced between the front door and a stage where the banjo player, an obese man, sat with buttocks overhanging either side of a stool.

I was astounded he, with fingers the size of corn cobs, could pick fast as a hummingbird beat wings, or so it seemed. He wore a top hat and black brocaded vest over a beer-stained white shirt with an open celluloid collar. Tufts of chest hair puffed from the open neck of the shirt, but he was so fat he had no neck unless that thing tapering outward from his ears to his shoulders had the necessary pipes somewhere inside.

The tables were half full and a few men leaned on or were seated at the bar. Most of them in the work clothes of men on the trail, but more than a couple were mountain dressed in fringed buckskins as were I and my two followers.

But all had eyes on the three soiled doves moving from table to table—one with hair as black as a raven's wing, one dirty blonde, and one dark red, same as a sorrel horse we once owned. Those that weren't watching them had eyes on another slim dove descending the stairs, with a ruffled looking trail hand following, whose hair was sticking out like he'd just sat bare-bottomed on a yellow jacket. Over blotched red cheeks stretched a silly grin that she ignored. He grinned like a jackass all the way down the stairs. She ignored him, eyeing the crowd like an eagle drifting over a muddy pond trying to decide which carp to sink its talons into.

Both Jasper and Alabama went straight to the bar, and before I could catch up, we each were being poured mugs of beer to sit beside small glasses of whiskey already in place.

"I don't—" I started to say, but Alabama jabbed me in the ribs, forgetting I guess that they were sore as if covered in carbuncles, and I gasped as he chastised me.

"Boy, you're in a pleasure house and by all that's holy, you're gonna join us with some of the nectar of the gods. I ain't never rode with no shotgun guard who's never dipped his wick. Drink up."

I nodded, hardly able to speak as my eyes were still trying to focus from being jabbed.

Lifting the beer, I only touched it to my lips.

"Now a shot of the corn," Jasper said and cackled.

So, I did the same with the whiskey. I was happy to be relieved of their attention as one of the ladies sidled up and eyed each of us in turn. She wore a sky-blue gown, not as regal as Mandy Mays' but fitted as tightly. Maybe even more so as the buttons down the bodice strained against her generous girth and I wouldn't have been surprised if one popped and hit me in the eye. She was older than my Ma, and not nearly as pretty, even if without her strange decoration.

"I suppose you highbinders ain't got a dollar for a token?" she said, with only half her reddened lips upturned. Then she eyed me reproachfully as I was staring.

"What the hell are you staring at, whippersnapper?" she demanded.

She had tattoos on each cheek, from mid-cheek to jaw line, wiggles as if the artist was trying to display a pair of snakes that had crawled down out of her eye sockets.

"Not a thing, ma'am," I managed.

"The hell you're not. You're admiring my pet snakes, right?"

"If you say so, ma'am," I again managed, in a low tone.

"It ain't for me to say, sonny. It's for you. So, what is it?"

"They are fine, ma'am. Just fine."

"The Mojave gave me them. Thought I'd be pretty as a speckled pup had I some snakes on my cheeks. They killed and scalped my ma and pa, don't ya know? I lived with 'em until I was rescued."

"No, ma'am, I surely didn't know."

Alabama, smiling, saved me. "So, lass, are you ready for a little roll in the hay."

She laughed at him. "We ain't got no hay except out in the barn, but if you can stand clean sheets and more important, have a token, I'm your huckleberry."

"Don't have one quite yet." He turned, swigged down his whiskey, and beat the little glass on the bar to get the burly bartender's attention. The man hurried his way, carrying a plain bottle, no label, of house corn. Alabama covered his glass with one hand so the man couldn't pour and flopped a dollar coin on the bar with the other. "A ticket to paradise," he said, and the bartender nodded and reached in his pocket and placed a brass token on the bar, returning to his pocket with the coin.

"That'll get you fifteen minutes, pilgrim. Old as you are it may take that long to get it up. Don't overstay your welcome."

The much older Alabama growled right back at him, "Sonny, had I not had other pleasures on my mind, I'd likely slap you silly 'til the hogs come home." But he didn't wait for a challenge, grabbed the tattooed lady and headed for the stairway.

Jasper moved over to sit next to me. "You got a dollar, younger?" he asked.

"I do, but not to buy a case of the pox. Besides, I hurt so dang bad I probably couldn't…uh, whatever."

Jasper laughed, then we both realized the place had gone silent. I turned to see one of the men, a barrel-chested man in the canvas trousers, woolen shirt, and floppy hat of a farmer, who'd been out on the porch with Mandy Mays. He stood with his arms extended toward the doorway, his palms out as if trying to ward something off.

I cut my eyes to the west window where a plain farm lady in a dust cap and ankle-length gingham dress stood outside…with a double barrel shouldered, both barrels fully cocked.

9

"Henry, you lied to me one too many times. Cursed is the cheat, Malachi One Fourteen," the woman with the scattergun screamed, and it rang through the room where even the banjo player had silenced.

Mandy Mays, still outside on the porch, yelled as loudly, "Don't you dare shoot that fool through my glass. That came all the way from Boston."

But the woman's gaze didn't waver.

The man, in a quivering voice, yelled back, "Sarah, if you do not forgive others their sins, your Father will not forgive your sins, Matthew Six Fifteen."

He began to back up, hands still extended, as she yelled again, trembling both voice and extended arms, "Truly I tell you, everyone who sins is a slave to sin, John Eight Thirty-four."

He stuttered, his face now gone white, his smile belying his fear and tight as snake lips, "Did you hear me? But if you do not forgive others their sins, your father will not forgive yours, Matthew...don't do it, Sarah. You'll burn in hell."

"I'm already burning in hell, living with you," she

screamed and fired a barrel, blowing mullions and four panes of glass away. Even those patrons not in the line of fire were splattered by shards of window glass and splinters of wood. And she was a fine shot, even though he was only five paces away. The shot took him mid chest and blew him back across a table, scattering men, chairs, drinks, and playing cards.

But she wasn't through. She swung the shotgun at the nearest soiled dove, the thin girl who'd just descended the stairs and was searching for her next token.

"Jezebel!" the woman he'd called Sarah yelled. "Dove hell. You're a bloody buzzard," and fired again.

The girl was taken flush on a shoulder and spun away, slinging blood on those near. One of the men standing behind her was also hit and took a few pellets in the throat. He windmilled his arms as he stumbled backwards, then went to the floor.

The girl sunk to her knees, holding her shattered shoulder with the other hand, screaming so loud I was tempted to cover my ears. Then she slid to her back on the floor as another dove ran to the bar, jerked a towel, returned and pressed it to the shattered, shredded shoulder. But the blood could not be stopped and puddled around her.

There was no helping the man who'd taken the full blast to the chest. He had already stopped blowing blood-bubbles and was still.

Finally, the others in the room recovered, and several yelled, "Get her, get that murdering bitch." Several men charged outside and soon had her stretched out like Jesus on the cross.

Mandy Mays strode to her and speared her in the chest with a finger, "Damn you, damn you, that was a forty-dollar window."

I couldn't help but be taken aback. One on the floor

dead, two likely dying, and the woman was yelling about her window. I'm beginning to wonder if I'll ever understand what some call human nature. I'm beginning to think it's human nasty.

Then again, maybe a brothel is the wrong place to judge.

"Hang her. Get a rope," several of the men began to scream.

"There's a fine white oak right outside," Mandy Mays yelled.

"It ain't enough he was here. He was messing with his own daughter," the woman screamed. That quieted the crowd again, but not for long as they took up the cries more fervently.

So, she spat on the porch and condemned them. "Don't any of you have any common decency?"

It was Mandy Mays who answered, "No one gives a damn you killed your cheatin' husband, but you shot one of my girls and one of my payin' customers. That wasn't called for."

"I have the wisdom of God to administer justice, Kings...Kings Three," the woman mumbled, then began sobbing, her head hanging.

"Just because I run a whorehouse don't mean I don't know the Bible," Mandy Mays shouted, "Thou shalt not kill."

The woman looked up, now with fire in her eyes. "Then I shan't be hung," she said, glaring from man to man.

"The hell you won't," Mandy Mays yelled, spittle flying from her colored lips. "Hang her. Do the law's work or you'll never visit Mandy Mays' Pleasure Parlor again." Several men dragged her down the steps while one ran to his horse for a lariat.

In moments, he'd flung the loop over a limb, and without tying the thirteen turns had the simple slip knot over her head. Not on a horse, she was merely standing waiting to be hoisted. Men, on either side, held her in place, while another bound her wrists behind her.

We'd all crowded outside. I stood between Jasper and Alabama and looked from one to the other. "Are we gonna stand for this?" I asked.

Jasper, to his credit, looked disgusted, but merely shrugged. "Ain't our fight," he mumbled.

"My pa told me right was always my fight. She seems a pious woman, even if that was no pious act. And her getting a trial is what's right."

"Too late," Alabama said, as they hoisted her high, kicking as her eyes bulged and she strangled. She wet herself and it puddled in the mud beneath her. I felt totally disgusted and felt as if I should vault the railing, run and hoist her, but then the kicking stopped.

Had one of my mules kicked me in the chest, I couldn't have felt hollower.

I guess both Alabama and Jasper sensed my urge to run and hoist her, as both held tightly onto my arms.

"Settle down, younger," Alabama said, and I felt the blood rush from my chest, expelled a long breath I guess I'd been holding and suddenly felt totally exhausted. As if I'd run all this way from the Snake River.

"Let's go," I managed.

"That's a fine idea," Jasper said, and led us down the stairs. We walked, unhurried in complete silence, back to our camp near the Brown's barn where Chang and Stadt awaited, both standing with hands on hips, looking curious.

Tennison strode up from the wagon encampment the same time we did.

"What the hell happened at the brothel?" Stadt asked.

Tennison muttered, "The wagon camp was up in arms as if about to be attacked by hostiles. I found it a good time to retreat."

I went to find my bedroll, as Jasper and Alabama explained the events.

I'm glad I didn't have to participate in the explanations as merely thinking of it made me sick to my stomach. It seemed a long time before I was blessed with sleep, as thinking of it was hard to avoid.

And when I did doze off, I was quickly awakened by the shouts of more than two dozen men and a few women stomping by. They were carrying rifles, shouting, and shaking their fists.

Looks like the night's excitement is not over.

10

As tired and sore as I was, I couldn't help pulling on my trousers and boots and tagging along after Stadt, Alabama, Jasper and Tennison. Chang was instructed by Stadt to stay behind and guard the camp—which meant guard all those wrapped fifteen-pound loaves he'd buried in the barn's loose hay.

The mob leading us, a few of them carrying lanterns, was obviously crazed with anger, and even more so as we neared the brothel. The lady who'd been called Sarah was still hanging beneath the large limb of the huge white oak. And anyone would be revolted by the sight. Her tongue was distended, and her eyes wide as if her last sight was of the sonorous tongues of Hell's hot fire licking on her feet and calves.

A few men, now a drunken clutch of wavering fools, were gathered on the porch eying the macabre sight of a woman hanging, her skirts wet with urine, the smell from her released sphincter no more pleasant than the view.

As the mob neared, the men on the porch eyed them with well-deserved suspicion and fingered their holstered guns or those shoved in their belts.

A large man with a body like a hogshead barrel, a full gray beard, and an unruly head of hair that reminded me of pictures of Moses in one of Ma's books, stepped forward a couple of paces ahead of the others, remaining the same distance from the lowest step.

"My name is Brother Horatio Luke Silverstein. Who ordered and who participated in this hanging? This outrage against all that's holy and legal."

Those on the porch looked from one to another, wondering who was going to step forward. No one did.

Then Mandy Mays pushed through the door. "What's this?" she snapped, pointing at the crowd below, many of who had sidearms in hand and long arms shouldered.

"This," the bearded man said, "is redemption. You have murdered our sister."

"Murdered, my sweet ass," Mandy Mays yelled. "That woman shot her man down, murdered one of my ladies who was sweet as honey, and a paying customer who just bled out on my floor from holes shot in his neck. Which of you are going to pay for my window and for cleaning my establishment?"

The bearded man stepped forward to the step, glaring up at the woman with carrot-colored hair. "It's time for you to clear this den of wickedness and damnation out. Vacate it or face the consequence."

Mandy Mays turned to the men on the porch. "Shoot them sons-a-bitches if they take a step closer."

But rather than continue to face the mob, the men on the porch, elbowed around her. With hands held far from weapons, they descended the steps and moved off. Some to horses tied to a nearby rail, some afoot.

"Damn cowards," Mandy Mays yelled after them. Then she moved to the blown away window and yelled inside through the opening. "I need help out here. Bring your weapons. This rabble is threatening me...us...this place."

A few men inside walked to the door and window, looked out at the mob covering the yard, then faded back. It seemed as much as they valued the wares, they didn't value them enough to risk life and limb.

"This be your last warning," gray beard said. Then he pointed to where three men had cut the lariat and were lowering the woman. "Leave the premises or face the fires of Hell."

Mandy Mays actually laughed, but it rang hollow, then she yelled, "And who the hell do you think you are, fat man? You ain't the Lord God and you ain't gonna judge us."

The big man shrugged then turned to his followers. "Now!" he yelled.

Mandy Mays screamed as a dozen coal oil lamps sailed through the air, three landing on the porch and washing the surface and lower front wall with flame.

She spun and fled inside, her trailing skirt afire.

Most of the lanterns smashed against the wall of the two-story log structure, but two smashed through upper story windows.

I suddenly was sickened by the fact I'd followed along. Men and a couple of soiled doves escaped at a run through the front door and braved the flames to make the front yard, where they were pummeled to the ground with heavy revolvers and gun butts. Two managed to run the gauntlet and fled into the nearby woods. More than a dozen men poured out the rear entrance, where two plank privies stood several steps from the building. Two of the men escaping turned and dropped to a knee, shouldered long arms, and fired indiscriminately into the crowd.

"Let's get the hell out of here," Stadt, who'd stayed a

good ten paces behind us, yelled at the rest of us. Then I realized Alabama was holding his stomach and blood flowed through his fingers.

He staggered a few steps then fell face first. I ran to him, and he grumbled, "Didn't even see who the hell shot me."

"Help me," I yelled at our fleeing party. Jasper and Tennison returned while Stadt ignored us and moved on fifty or more feet. We hoisted Alabama to his feet, and with his arms over Jasper and Tennison's shoulders, we headed for our camp.

But we didn't stop there and continued on a hundred paces to the most impressive dwelling in Brownsville, the two-story home of the Browns. We had heard that Mrs. Brown was an excellent nurse.

After banging on the door hard enough to wake the dead, it was minutes before Mr. Brown arrived at the front door.

And before he did, Alabama muttered to Jasper, "You got...you got all my weapons...and folderol, old friend. Bury me deep...real deep...so the critters don't get at me."

Mr. Brown opened his door and stepped out, seeing the wounded man.

"Inside," he said, and yelled back over his shoulder. "Missus Brown, we got a hurt man here." Then he looked over us. "What the devil?" he exclaimed, and we all turned to see the flames, now a roaring conflagration.

"They burned the brothel," I managed.

"Who?" he asked.

"The wagoners, 'cause them at the bawdy house hung a woman from the train."

"What the devil?" Mr. Brown said again. "Why?"

"Shot her husband, a dove and killed a customer."

He sighed deeply, then turned his attention back to

Jasper. Then studied him closely. "That man doesn't seem to need nursing," he said.

Jasper's head hung. Stadt reached over and put two fingers alongside Jasper's neck. Then he shook his head. "Dead as a damn snake stomped by a mule," he said, then turned to Mr. Brown. "Sorry to be a bother. Y'all got a buryin' place."

Brown nodded, "About a hundred yards out behind the barn, a fine little knoll any of us would be proud to occupy. You'll see the crosses. It's two dollars for a plot. Don't put him inside the little fenced in area. That's for family."

"The hell you say, two dollars," Stadt snapped. "We'll plant him yonder down the trail."

"Suit yourself," Mr. Brown said. "I'll want you to write out a statement on the morrow to send to the territorial judge in Oregon City. We don't take dead lightly. This is a civilized village."

I couldn't help myself and had to speak up as he was closing the door. "If this is civilized, I'd hate to see wild and woolly." But he merely shut the door.

11

Come first light, the last load we hoisted was Alabama draped over his skittish horse. As we rode out south along the Oregon Trail, skirting the wagon train who were packing up, ignoring Mr. Brown's order to report and write our observations, we passed a couple of fellas who were mounted but merely standing and staring at the distant smoldering blackened ruins of what had been Mandy Mays' pride and joy.

I reined up near them. "Everybody get out?" I asked.

One looked back over his shoulder. "Y'all with that wagon train?"

"No, sir. We're on the trail, heading south, all the way from Lewiston up on the Snake."

"Then you should know more than a dozen burned to death. Them rooms upstairs was full."

"Mandy Mays?" I asked.

"She must have went up with her joint. No one's seen her about. You got a dead man there?" He pointed at Alabama, draped over the horse.

I was tempted to say, 'no, he just likes to ride that'a'way,' but I contained myself. "Yes, he took a stray shot from some careless fool."

"Humph," the man said, then tipped his hat. "Stay safe out there. Word is the Paiutes and the Modocs are on the run."

"Thanks. We'll dang sure try."

Two miles south of Brownsville, we came on a soft meadow, well off the trail, full of belly-deep grass. On a little high spot, Tennison, Jasper, and Chang took turns digging a grave. When they were three feet into the loam, Stadt yelled at them.

"We ain't got time to dilly dally. Get him planted and let's get down the trail."

Jasper, who was on our little shovel, looked up and he wasn't looking happy. "Mister Stadt, Alabama said to bury him deep. I'm gonna bury him six feet under. If you don't like taking the time, you just ride on ahead."

"Fine, you finish that up and we'll be dividin' the old boy's goods up. I'll have first choice and I'll take his horse and—"

"Stadt," Jasper snapped, cutting him off. "All here heard Alabama say all'a his goods, critter, firearms, and folderol goes to me. I guess you didn't hear that, but you're a'hearin' it now."

"That ain't the way it's done on the trail, Jasper," Stadt said, his voice loud and certain.

"If that's what you're thinkin'…"

"It damn sure is."

"If that's what you're thinking, Stadt, then we'll be a while longer."

"Why the hell…"

"Cause I gotta start another hole soon as I finish this'n."

"What the hell for?" Stadt ask, his voice still strong.

"For you, cause you ain't taking what my friend here wanted me to have."

Stadt was quiet for several seconds as the two men stared at each other, then Stadt turned to Tennison. "You hear Alabama will his goods to Jasper?"

Tennison looked at Stadt as if he was something very smelly that he'd stepped in but said in a level voice. "We all heard it, Stadt. Maybe you were distracted?"

"Guess I was," he mumbled, then walked away to a bush just off the trail and relieved himself, buttoned up, and returned to plop down on a fallen log and watch the men dig.

He stretched, yawned and seemed totally unaffected by Jasper's threat.

I offered to help dig, but Jasper had watched me move about enough to know I was still pained by bruised and maybe even broken ribs, and he refused. Tennison relieved him and he sat with me a minute while dirt flew from the grave.

"You knew Alabama a long time?" I asked.

"We trapped and explored with Joe and Joel Walker back in thirty-two, then with Meek and Bill Craig to California. So, we done saw the elephant together many times. I wish I could haul his body back to Missouri and would. But he was hell on doing what he said he'd do, and we both signed on with this Scaramouch. Old Alabama would haul my oats if'n I didn't finish what we set out to do."

"Scaramouch?" I asked, never having heard the term.

"That would be a boastful coward."

"Stadt?"

"Don't worry, younger. Tennison here," and Tennison looked up from his work and gave us a nod, and Jasper continued, "is a man of his word and damn handy with that fancy Sharps. And that Celestial, Chang, is hell on wheels with that hatchet. But he don't depend only on it.

I've seen him with the cold iron in hand and he'll shoot a cigar outta your chompers at fifty yards. No savage will be shooting him in the back cause he's runnin'. And you seem right handy yourself. Less'n we're overrun with dozens of savages, we'll finish our job and if Stadt don't abide by our agreement, we'll skin the slackard and tack his hide to the outhouse wall."

I had to laugh at that.

Jasper continued, "That right, Mister Tennison?"

Tennison stopped his digging and glanced over, "You don't have to worry about Stadt. I signed him on, and I can give him the boot."

"Good enough," Jasper said, and reached for the shovel. "Gimme that and I'll finish up." Then he turned to me, "Mister Zane, gather up some rocks to line this grave if the effort don't pain you too much. I don't want the critters to get at my friend."

We wrapped Alabama in a tarp, so we wouldn't be throwing dirt in his face, and buried him six feet under the loam. Stadt never rose from his seat on a distant log, while both Tennison and Jasper said a few words over Alabama. After Jasper finished quoting the Twenty-third Psalm, we mounted up and continued.

When we stopped for some jerky and hardtack and to blow the stock and let them wet their lips in a small trickle, I could help but ask Jasper, "You use lots of big words?"

"You ain't never gonna stop learning, younger, be it about the critters, the savages, the weather, one another, or words and such. The more you know, the better you live. I always got me a book and though you don't see me reading on this trip yet, you will."

"What book are you carrying?"

"Song of Ilion, some call it the Iliad. Writ by a fella

name of Homer. Lived a long time ago. Old Greek boy writing in a poetic form about the Trojan War. When I finish, I'll loan it to you, you promise to treat it careful. I got some scribblin' in the back about things, words and such, I want to know more about."

"And how are you gonna do that?"

"Hell, boy, ain't you never hear'd of a library. I get around one every couple of years and, if they let me in, might spend me a week diggin' around for things I hanker to know more about."

I could only nod. My pa told me to never judge a book by its cover, and I'd sure as the devil misjudged this old, unshaven, rough-dressed, mountain man. I'm gonna try and remember not to make that mistake again.

He's a learned man, but I'd already seen he's all teeth and claws when it comes to a fight. So, one don't fight shy of the other. Tennison, too, seems to be well educated and looks it. And fights like a wolverine when necessary.

And I'm glad it's so, and that I'm riding with Tennison, Chang, and old Jasper. If what that rider back aways is right, and the Modoc and Paiute are riled up, the fighting is a long way from over.

12

That night, after we'd had a trail supper of the last of the bear loin, beans that Chang cooked with nearly as many greens he'd picked mixed in, and biscuits, we plopped it down by a low fire. As the man we'd seen watching the smoldering brothel had mentioned Modocs and Paiutes, I thought it might behoove me to know something about the folks whose country we'd be riding into, so I asked.

"Jasper, you've been in this Paiute and Modoc country before?"

"Alabama and I joined up with Joe Walker back in Osage, Missouri, way back in '32, when we was young and full of piss and vinegar—"

"Like you ain't now," I said. Tennison, who'd joined in, and I laughed.

"We headed out with more'n a hundred men. Some ducked out along the way and we come on with forty but run into another twenty. When Walker said he was headed to California, and that President Jackson had pointed him that'a'way, they joined up. If Old Hickory wanted it done, most of us fell in line. And it was a good thing we became sixty as we crossed paths with hundreds of Paiutes. They soon found they didn't want to tangle with white men with long guns as we fertilized the plain with plenty of Paiute blood. We headed on into what's now California and run into some Modocs along the way. I wouldn't be a damn bit surprised if they don't have their own long guns by this time. Seems there's always some damn fool who'll trade muzzle loaders, lead, and powder for furs, and don't care if others pay with blood."

"So," I asked, "when will we run into these Paiutes and Modocs?"

"Likely it'll be Paiutes first…by the by. Paiutes is Utes who live by water, or so the name means. Likely we'll see Modocs when we get in sight of the Sierras and the Klamaths."

"Sierras?" I asked.

"The mountain range on the east edge of Californey."

"And the Klamaths?" I asked.

"Them are across the north of the new state tying them coast mountains to the high Sierras. We'll enter California kinda between the two. Fact is we might meet up with Klamath, Bannock, and Shoshone red men as well. All of 'em a little irritable about us wandering around their hunting grounds."

"Will they let us pass peaceful?" I asked.

"They's times when you can walk right by a rattle-snake and he'll pay you little mind. Next time he'll come at you like he ain't et in a year. Who the devil knows?"

As I lay in my bedroll that night, trying to grab some sleep as I still had 3:00 a.m. guard duty, I couldn't help but think about a word Ma had taught us on the trip out. Tenuous, and that's what I figured life is. Tenuous—frag-ile, weak. That's what life is. Just a little over a day ago, I was laughing and jesting with Alabama, and now he's feeding the worms. And all those other folks who were pretty much minding their own business, whoopin' it up in Mandy May's? Now a dozen of them are toast. Including Mandy Mays if the old boy astride his horse was right.

Besides the sadness of losing who'd become a friend, the whole affair made me ride a bit lighter in the saddle. My eyes are doing a better job of scanning the country ahead and to the side as we plod along.

Getting laid out cold seems easy enough in this wild country, hardly a road between the Oregon Trail and the California Trail, but plenty of ways to meet your maker.

We were making good time and had passed more than a hundred wagons on the trail before it turned east, and we left the two track and continued south. We were again on game trails and having to pick our way. Jasper seemed to have a sixth sense about where the country would open up and where we could pass easily. I had great faith in him, and was happy to note that old, tall, thin Stadt seemed content to let Jasper lead out.

We plodded out of the pines into what Jasper said was out of Oregon Territory and into Utah territory—high desert country. Jasper said it was the edge of the Black Rock Desert—it was properly named—and we'd come across a branch of the California Trail soon. Strange country, occasionally a mud flat, broken and curled chunks, then sage punctuated with a layer of black rock, then a wide plane of nothing but sand. Inhospitable, more so than any country I'd seen since leaving Missouri. In the distance, I see what first made me nervous as I thought it plumes of smoke from Indian campfires. Jasper informed me it was hot springs and only steam rising. The Black Rock is on the northwest edge of the Great Basin, so called as no rivers run out of the huge sink in the center of the west.

Jasper won't take the California Trail as this branch of it runs southeast to northwest, and it's southwest we'd be heading. A right angle to the trail. Sage billows belly deep to the horses and mules, like huge bubbles of blue green in areas and has to be picked through, so it's a zigzag route we follow. But on occasion, lots of good graze brushed the bellies of the horses and mules. Crossings were no problem with only the occasional trickle of water. Jasper, while ranging ahead of us, downed a huge bull elk—said there was a herd of over one hundred—that gave us fresh meat that would feed us more than a week. All was going well…too well I worried.

I feared my two dollars a day was coming way too easily.

It was a week of easy riding, having to cross a stream or two where the stock had to swim, but we'd had no wrecks or lost any gear. I knew all was going too smoothly as I hadn't had my long arms out of their scabbards or my Colt from its holster, when I spotted a tendril of smoke, not steam, in the distance.

"You see that?" I yelled up to Jasper who was picking our trail and staying close. We could see miles in any direction, so he wasn't concerned with us riding into trouble without any warning. Unless the savage was creeping through the sage leaving his mount behind.

Jasper reined back to where I was leading my mule string. "I been watching that smoke for the last half hour. We're gonna swing way to the west. I'd guess that be Paiute. I'm surprised this time of year they ain't farther south where they parley around a lake you can't hardly see across. Pyramid Lake, as I recall, as they be a pointy island in the middle reminds folks of drawings of those big ol' things the ancients built in Egypt in Moses time."

"I'd like to see that," I said.

"Not this trip, younger. We'll be swinging too far west. In a few days, we'll be entering our thirty-first state." He gave me a wink, "You got to be careful or your horse will trip over the gold nuggets."

I laughed. "I'll watch careful."

Then I got serious again as I looked to the southeast and saw a line of riders reined up a quarter mile away.

"Looks like we didn't ride far enough west," I said, and pointed.

Jasper nodded. "Let's hope they're fat and sassy and not wantin' to get their bellies full of lead trying to relieve us of our goods."

"From your lips to God's ears," I said and meant it.

Stadt who was not leading a string, as usual, galloped up and joined us. "What do you make of it, Jasper?"

"Ain't making my day rosy," he replied.

"How many you think?"

"Well, sir, them Paiutes are two thousand strong or more as a tribe. I make that bunch at twenty or so, but that don't mean a thing."

"Are we gonna fort up?"

"They be a little ridge up a ways. Hopefully, water in a cut there. It's a mite early, but I'd say camp there where we got the high ground, such as it is."

As we talked, it was obvious we'd been seen, as the Indians strung out and were coming our way.

"Should we run for it?" Stadt asked.

"Dragging these here loaded-down mules? Not unless you want them loaves spread all over the desert. With luck, all they want to do is parley and maybe get a few trinkets. You know where you packed them axe heads?"

"I left them after we lost those two mules."

"Well, sir," Jasper said, and sounded a little worried, "that likely wasn't your best decision."

"But it's made. Let's get to that ridge and fort up."

We gigged our stock to a fast walk until we topped the

little rise, which luckily did have water in a trickle below a cut.

We led our stock to a nearby low spot and quickly made a corral of line and lead ropes tied together and strung from the tallest sage. It would hold until they munched all the graze or got thirsty. Or until the savages raised hell and scared them to jumping and running.

The packs and panniers, saddles and blankets, made a fair makeshift stockade, and then we hunkered down and waited.

13

Our wait wasn't long.

Four of the savages rode out ahead of the others. Only two carried muzzle loaders. The other two had spears as long as the Indians were tall, but seated and pointing upright. They didn't seem to be painted for war, although their horses sported red and yellow handprints, and they wore feathers in their hair and headbands.

We'd left our stock loosely saddled, and Jasper moved to the makeshift corral and recovered his tall sorrel. He sucked up the latigo and led the gelding over.

"I believe I'll borrow me a scattergun," he said, and I handed him one I'd stuffed into the lashes on one of the packs. I still had one and my Colts, and he was riding out to parley.

"You want company?" I asked.

"I'm pulling up fifty or sixty paces out, well within range. You fellas make it plain you've laid down on them. So y'all stay put. Make sure none of them left behind are moving around to flank us."

"Go with God," Tennison said as he settled down resting the Sharps on a pack. He waved me over and I sidled up next to him. He slipped a hand in a coat pocket and handed me a little two-shot Derringer. "Boy, this is a last resort. Pull once and the top barrel fires, second pull is the bottom. I've seen what these savages will do they catch you alive. Save the last shot for yourself."

"Thank you, I guess," I said, and gave him a weak smile, then asked, "How about you?"

"I got a spare in my other pocket. That's yours to keep."

"I'm obliged," I said, and started back just as Jasper gigged his sorrel.

Jasper nodded, then yelled over his shoulder at us, "Hope the good Lord is with all of us," and gave heels to his animal, picking his way through the sage at a trot until he reined up at the distance he'd said was within range.

Four of us remained behind, and four Paiute approached and reined up ten paces from where Jasper sat with the scattergun across his thighs.

We could not hear the exchange, and I guess I wouldn't have understood it even had I been able. I broke the Derringer and checked the load and the caps, then stuffed it into my belt.

It didn't look as if there was a great disagreement going on between the Indians and Jasper, in fact, it looked pretty cordial. It was only moments before Jasper spun his horse and headed back. The four Indians remained.

When he neared, he yelled at Chang, "You still got a hindquarter of that elk?"

"That's all I have," Chang replied.

"Fetch it, and a pound of sugar."

Chang nodded, and did so. Jasper sheathed the scattergun, replaced it across his thighs with the hindquarter, hung the sack of sugar over his saddle horn, spun and returned to the parley.

He dropped the sack of sugar and kicked the hindquarter off into a sage. Gave the Indians a casual salute and reined his horse around. One of the savages raised his muzzle loader and fired as soon as he had Jasper's back.

It was a mistake, as one of the Indians jumped from his mount to recover the goods but didn't make it as Tennison's Sharps bucked in his hands, and the Indian flew back across another sage. Tennison yelled as he reloaded another paper cartridge, "That devious son of a she dog won't back shoot anyone again."

Chang, Stadt, and I fired at the same time as the remaining Indians tried to escape. One of them slipped from horseback and went face first onto the black rocks. We all were pouring powder, balls, and jamming wads in our weapons. I was ahead of Stadt and Chang, but not nearly as quick on the reload as Tennison. As I put another cap on the nipple, Tennison was taking a breath and holding it. The Indians were over a hundred yards and escaping at a gallop, but straight away, which wasn't much in the way of evading the Sharps. It bucked again in his arms. One of the remaining Indians seemed to lose his way, and his mount swung out to the left. Then as it jumped a sage, the rider was thrown and didn't get up or struggle from tangling in a big sagebrush.

Jasper was leaning over the sorrel's neck but coming at a trot back to our scrimmage line. He was not reining the horse, but the animal was finding his own way. He jumped the little trickle of water below the ridgeline, and Jasper tumbled from the saddle. The sorrel climbed the face of the little ridge and headed for his chums in the corral.

Tennison and I clambered down the bank, got Jasper up with arms over our shoulders, climbed back up and lay him on saddle blankets Chang had spread on the sand.

"Get back to your positions," Stadt yelled.

But I could see Jasper was shot though the side and needed tending. Besides, Tennison and the Sharps were our first line of defense. "Go," I said to Tennison, "I'll do what I can."

"Filthy lying savages," Jasper said, as I jerked his buckskin shirt up, packed his wounds with wadding material I used for my muzzle loaders, then fetched a spare shirt from my haversack and bound it around his middle to compress the wound.

"Get your ass…" Stadt snapped at me.

But I interrupted him, "I'm tending his wound. He'll bleed out if'n I don't."

"Get it done," Stadt yelled.

I was tempted to assist the Indians by shooting Stadt myself. But Jasper interrupted my thought, "He's right. Get on your rifle."

So, I did, but kept glancing back to make sure my nursing was working, and I'd quelled the bleeding. The wound was below the ribs and away from his backbone, entering from the back and exiting four inches from his navel. With luck it didn't clip a gut for if it did there'd be little chance of saving him.

Of course, our first effort had to be saving us all.

The savages had disappeared into a ravine over a rise and were nowhere in sight.

"Jake," Tennison yelled at me. "You keep a sharp eye out for signs of them. We're going to build up our defenses."

We had two axes and a shovel, and to my surprise, Stadt pitched right in chopping sage and piling it so we couldn't be seen but still had plenty of shooting ports. They worked for an hour, even surrounding the stock with seven or eight feet of piled sage. It both kept the stock out of sight and helped fence them in.

When they were happy with the fortifications, such as they were, Tennison and Stadt returned to lookout and we took stations where we could observe the horizon in all directions.

I took the opportunity to move back to where Jasper lay on his bed of horse blankets.

"How you doin'?" I asked quietly as his eyes were closed, and I didn't want to wake him, but didn't as he opened them and gave me a wink.

"Hell, younger, I been shot through both legs and got a grove in my shoulder you could park a cigar in. They ain't got this old hound dog yet. Get your young eyes back to work and make sure they ain't sneaking up on us."

"Will they come at night?"

"Most of 'em believe their soul will wander the darkness forever, they give it up at nighttime. So, I'd guess you don't have to worry 'til dawn."

"Rest easy," I said, but could tell he was hurting something awful.

We decided to stand guard in two-hour shifts, two at a time, one out near the stock, one moving from position to position at the other three spots on the compass.

We kept a cold camp, not wanting to backlight anyone with a fire.

I hoped Jasper was right. If they came at night, with all the heavy sage, they could sneak up and be on us, the seventeen or so of them who were left, before we could do much in the way of defense.

14

We awoke, Chang and I, as Tennison and Stadt had the last watch, to a stiff wind coming out of the mountains far to the west. It was hard enough that brush occasionally blew overhead. Chang set about digging a small hole for a cookfire and got coffee boiling while I went to the corral and led the stock, two at a time, to the little trickle at the bottom of the cut that we'd built our fortifications atop.

I was not comfortable being even a few feet in front of our wall of packs and panniers, but the horses and mules had to have water. The sun was over the horizon to the east before I was finished, and I was somewhat surprised I hadn't had to scramble back to cover with savages on my tail.

But so far, so good. At least I hadn't had to put that Derringer up to my temple and fire my last shot.

We sat tight until midmorning, watching the skyline, searching the wide expanse of sage covered ground in all directions.

Nothing.

Hawks, meadowlarks, a skein of ducks high overhead, but not a savage in sight.

"You suppose those three we shot cured them of sucking eggs?" Tennison said, scanning in all directions.

Jasper lifted his head. "Them boys know where we come from so know the way we're headed. A couple of miles ahead, maybe three or four, we go into a canyon and head due west against the flow of a little creek. She gets tight as a tick in a lamb's tail in that hole, but it's the way into the pass twixt the Sierras and the Klamath Range."

"No other way?" Stadt asked.

"Probably lots of ways. But damned if I know them, and I'd hate to get halfway to Poverty Flats and the headwaters of the Sacramento and have to turn back. I need to mend a while…"

"The hell you say," Stadt growled. "We ain't hangin' around here waitin' for the rest of them Paiutes to gather up and come for our hair. We're movin' on, come mornin' at the latest."

"Have a nice trip," Tennison said.

"You gonna lead eight mules?" I asked.

Stadt turned to Chang. "You with me?" he asked.

"You want die. Five men not enough. Two die for sure."

Stadt was getting red in the face, standing with fists at his side.

"And if it was you hurt, Mister Stadt?" I asked.

"It ain't me and I signed on to get this load through. Waiting for Willoby to heal up, or die, ain't my job." He turned to Tennison, "Ain't that right, Tennison?"

Tennison had been staring out into the sage, but turned to answer, just as an arrow sliced into his neck from the side.

Stadt, Chang and I dove for the cover of our pack and sage stockade as a half dozen other arrows whistled by and disappeared into the sage or stuck in the sand.

Tennison was on his back, his hands on the arrow that

had gone through his neck, the fletched end on one side, the bloodied arrowhead on the other.

I scrambled back to him, staying low, and reached down and busted the fletched end off and pulled it on through. But that may have only hastened his demise. His hands went to both sides of his neck desperately trying to stem the bleeding, but blood gushed through his fingers.

He was trying to speak, but only gurgling.

"Get back here," Stadt yelled.

"He's dying," I yelled back.

"And you holdin' his hand won't keep it from happenin'. Get your rifle up here, now!"

I knew that the big arteries in his neck were cut, and he only had seconds to live. Against Stadt's admonition, I took Tennison's hand and held it until his eyes stopped moving and the blood stopped gushing through his fingers. His eyes took on the dead sheen of someone whose soul has flown.

I got a horrible taste in my mouth. Another friend gone. This one among the most admirable men I'd ever met, or certainly worked with.

"Damn your hide," Stadt yelled at me.

I dropped Tennison's limp hand and returned to the portal I'd been using.

We waited quietly while several more arrows flew overhead, and never saw so much as a feather in the sage beyond. The savages stayed out of sight and lobbed arrows. None came within three paces of us. Then I heard the pained whinny of a mule or horse, then a shrill heehaw that identified the animal as mule.

Staying low, I made my way across our little camp and the five paces beyond to the corral. I picked out a mule in the middle of the herd whose eyes were wide, and I could see him shivering. I slipped into the roped in area and the animals parted enough that I saw the arrow protruding from the animal's flank.

I tried to slip between them to grip the arrow shaft and pull it free, but they continued to move, circling the tight corral. I spent half my time looking over my shoulder to make sure a savage was not pulling a bow with me in sight. Then I had an idea. I was able to separate the wounded mule and a tall bay gelding—a horse any horseman would covet. I dropped the rope gate and shooed them out. Unfortunately, another mule followed before I could prevent it.

The three of them charged off into the sage to the east and I hurried back to my portal between packs and sage.

"What the hell," Stadt yelled, seeing the fleeing animals.

"It may be hell if those savages don't go after those animals," I said, praying my ploy would work.

The arrows stopped flying, and as I watched, a half-dozen savages crossed the low ridge over a hundred and fifty yards to the east. Then in moments, another hundred yards distant, a dozen savages rode out at a full gallop. They were pursuing our fleeing three head.

I walked over to where Jasper still lay, eyes closed, hands over the wound in his belly.

"Jasper, I'm gonna make a drag from that bear hide you skinned and we're gonna move out at least a mile or so. Maybe the Paiute will be convinced we've moved on."

"Better than waiting here to be scalped."

With that I yelled to Chang to help, and we dragged Tennison to the edge of the bank and over. Then with our little shovel, we collapsed the bank on top of his body, then threw as many stones as we could gather on the makeshift grave.

I mumbled what I could remember of the Twenty-third

Psalm and told him I was sorry we couldn't bury him correctly. But it was what it was.

The wind was still whistling. Stadt, Chang, and I worked like the devil was on our tail packing the remaining mules, saddling our horses, and me building a drag for Jasper. If we had some saplings near, I would rig a travois as I'd seen some of the plains Indians use, but we'd have nothing so fancy. We got Jasper half rolled and tied in the bear hide, with a line leading back on either side of my saddle. It was hell on my legs, but it also was what it was, and I had no choice.

The last thing I did was gather coals from Chang's fire and move to a pile of brush to the east of us. In moments, I had a fire roaring and the wind did the rest. A true grass and brush fire was chasing the savages. I doubted if they'd be coming back our way anytime soon. I remounted and set out. The trickle of water below the bank where we'd built our stockade was only an inch or so deep and four or five feet wide. I set out dragging Jasper right up the middle of the trickle.

Stadt grumbled as he had to lead two mules and Chang four. Two horses still ran free. I had all I could do to drag my load.

And the load with which we were entrusted was still with us.

But it was coming out of the southwest, the direction Jasper said we were going, and our best chance of not leaving track.

We rode into the wind and upstream, but when I glanced behind, the whole plain was afire. There was little question in my mind that the savages were hotfooting it, maybe literally, the opposite way from our trek.

And before we'd gone a mile, we were helped by the good Lord. The sky opened and it began a heavy rain.

Soon, I had to leave the trickle as I feared drowning Jasper as it deepened. By the time we reined up out of its cut, it was six inches deep and we were going upstream, where you'd normally think it would lessen.

The good news was the rain would put out the fire. The bad news was the rain would put out the fire. And we were all soaked to the bone.

To my great pleasure, after we moved up out of the ravine, we came on a two track, and only wagons make a two track.

"Likely Applegate Trail," Jasper managed to yell up to me.

"To California?" I yelled back.

"Yep, branch to California, branch to Oregon."

Things are going our way. Dang if it doesn't appear we left all those Paiutes behind.

Then I'm suddenly doubting my former conclusion. The hell of it is, there are more feathered and painted savages across the trail ahead, more than twice as many as we left behind. These are attired differently, but savages sure as Hell's hot.

15

We drew up. But there was no whipping up our horses in retreat. Leading mules precludes outrunning them. Dragging Jasper at more than a slow walk was out of the question.

We were coming into trees out of the high desert, and it had been my plan to stop and make a decent travois as bouncing along with only a bear skin betwixt Jasper and a bumpy and occasionally rocky trail was likely to beat him to death. Even if he didn't die from his wound. And he'd long ago decided he couldn't sit a saddle.

But the fellas in the trail ahead discouraged my progress, and conditions discourage my retreat. At more than a hundred paces away, they appeared peaceful enough. No weapons shouldered, bows without arrows notched.

Then to my great surprise, a white man in buckskins reined between them, followed by another. The Indians stayed while he picked his way down the wide trail and headed our way.

As they neared, he raised a hand, palm out, a sign of peace and I let out a long breath I'd been holding.

"Howdy, pilgrim," he said as he reined up. "I'm Jedidiah Philbert and this here is my brother Seth. Looks like you got a hurt man there?"

"Yes, sir. I'm Jake Zane, the gentleman behind me goes by Chang, and following him is Gunter Stadt." It pained me to add. "He's the leader of our outfit. On the drag is Jasper Willoby."

"Dang if it ain't. I have made Mister Willoby's acquaintance."

"And those fellas you're riding with," I motioned behind him at the Indians.

"Them are Okwannuchus, from up near Shasta. We been doing some trading."

"Peaceful?" I asked, still a little apprehensive.

"So far, they been having some run ins with the Modocs. You seen any?"

"No, sir. We just had a run in with the Paiute."

As we were talking, Stadt gigged his horse up alongside me.

"I'm Gunter Stadt, and I'll do the talkin' for this company."

Philbert gave him a tight smile. "Company?"

"We're less than we started."

"Seems so," Philbert said, then reined around Stadt to look down on Jasper.

"Jasper, it's Jed Philbert. What the devil you doin' laying about this time of day?"

"Philbert? Hell…" he gasped a little, "…ain't seen you since the rendezvous in Gingras."

"Yep, that was a fine meeting. Won me a five-shot pepperbox in a footrace."

"Don't imagine you got…got any sulphur," Jasper asked.

"No, but them Okwannuchu women seem to be fine

nurses. When we rode in, Seth had him a gaggle of boils under his arm, and they got him drained and dried in three days. Got us a camp another half mile ahead. If you'll trust your immortal soul to the squaws, I'd bet you'll be dancing a jig in a fortnight."

"Sittin' a saddle'll do," Jasper said.

"We ain't waitin' no fortnight," Stadt said. "I got business in San Francisco."

"Mister Stadt," I snapped, "again, if you want to lead seven mules yourself, then…"

"We'll give him a couple of days," Stadt said, then his jaw set hard, and his face reddened, but he said no more.

I turned back to Philbert. "How's the trail from here on?"

"You'll soon be on the Lassen Trail. Soon as you get down into the foothills past these high peaks, you'll think you're in London Town. Dang if we weren't passed by a half-dozen parties heading north until we got over the pass. Seems there's another gold discovery up Eureka way."

"We got no interest in gold," Stadt said quickly. "We just need to get on to San Francisco."

Philbert nodded. "Well, pilgrim, in forty miles or so you'll be into easy riding damn nigh all the way there. Fifteen or twenty days, with luck and should you not be besieged by highwaymen."

Philbert glanced down at my saddle scabbard. "I don't imagin' you'd be wantin' to trade that there Sharps?"

"No sir, willed to me by a friend we lost back aways."

"Too bad, I sure do fancy it."

"Wouldn't take all the gold in California for it," I said, with finality.

"Highwaymen?" Stadt asked, suddenly looking worried. Then he added. "They must be desperate if they'd hold up some fellas for some camp gear and mules."

"My friend, they's been more'n one hundred thousand hooligans and sojourners from every rat's nest in the world land and jump ship in San Francisco. They's near a thousand ships at anchor in the bay, with no one to man them. Every mother's son is in the hills with a pick and pan. And all of them ain't finding their riches the honest way." Then he laughed. "Let's get Mister Willoby where he can comfort himself."

They had a fine camp, more than twenty wickiups, bent willow, caulked mud, and covered with brush and skins, on the shore of what Philbert called Eagle Lake. The men were not as tall and handsome as some natives I'd seen on the plains, nor were the women lithe, and they were not modest about their breasts and exposed them freely. I soon discovered their diet was not appealing to me as they ate the inner bark of some trees and were not shy about popping the occasional grub or insect. They'd gathered baskets full of grubs along the shore of the lake, the result of some fly that bred there. Not appetizing to me, so long, at least, as I had jerky and hard tack. The men stood as tall as they could and seemed proud of themselves. They paid us little heed, except for the women who tended Jasper and his wounds.

I shared a wickiup with Jasper, wanting to watch over him, and making sure the women were doing him no harm—not that I would be sure one way or the other. They applied poultices of leaves and roots soaked in hot water. And he seemed to respond well.

As the Philberts were short of grub, and we were short two men, we shared ours. Stadt tried to employ them for the rest of the trip, but they declined, saying they were compiling caches of furs and had many bales hidden in the hills.

On the morning of the third day, I awoke to find Jasper moaning, and when I touched his forehead discovered it wet with sweat and him as hot as had he just climbed from a dip in a hot spring.

When the women checked in on their patient, they immediately changed the poultices and were soon forcing him to drink a broth they brewed on a fire just outside our skin-covered doorway.

By the time the sun was dipping over the mountains to the west, he was cooling off, unfortunately it was not from being well but from no longer breathing.

I was sick at heart. I like Chang, but he barely speaks my language, not that I've not learned a lot by merely watching what he gathers and cooks. But I learned from Jasper daily, as I'd learned from Alabama and Tennison. Tennison, I'd guess, was a man who'd get along in a wickiup or the White House, a pueblo or a palace. Like my ma and pa, he valued fine things, including manners, and, without embarrassing me, corrected mine upon occasion.

The Indians didn't seem to approve of our burying Jasper. Before we rode out on the fourth morning, I gave the women the smaller of two hunting knives I possessed, thanks to Tennison willing me one along with his other goods. I now was the proud owner of a Sharps, and the makings of another one hundred or more paper cartridges. Stadt had claimed Jasper's gear, and I didn't argue, even though he didn't divvy it up as even he'd claimed was common on the trail.

Tennison's Sharps and possibles bag full of paper cartridges and the makins', his fine black gelding of nearly seventeen hands, his black polished saddle as fine as any my pa had ever made, and a fine sharp hunting and skinning knife was more than I expected to own until I'd worked for many a year. So, I kept my dislike of Stadt quiet, as did Chang, for I knew he held the straw boss in disregard.

As we moved through the pass between the Sierras and the Klamaths, I couldn't help but be concerned about Stadt. He insisted on riding drag, not common for the captain of any horseback venture. I understood it when he feared taking the first arrow from the Paiutes, but the Philberts assured us the Modocs were far to the north. The boss seldom is interested in eating others' dust.

Was he planning something foul? He needed us, but we knew what we hauled, and he could soon hire many others who'd have no idea of our cargo. Maybe he had no plans to deliver it at all. Now that Tennison was no longer with us...I wonder...is Stadt starting to think it was fate that those most likely to oppose him were dead and gone?

He held Chang and me in little regard.

I hoped I didn't have to prove him wrong.

16

We passed a sign on the trail, now a two track, where it branched off pointing southeast to Rooptown Trading Post and Lumber Mill. But we kept on west, where the sign said, Feather River and then Leodocia—signs, I guess we're back in civilization. In less than one hundred miles, we'd be in California's great central valley. Less than two hundred miles south—easy riding I'm told then, except for the swamp land and mosquitos—down the Sacramento River to the city of the same name, Sacramento City, then to the gold rush boomtown of San Francisco. I've never seen the great Pacific Ocean, so I'm eager to do so.

We were two hard days to the beautiful mountain river said to be the headwaters of the Feather River, here only little more than a stream. It's said to dump into the Sacramento. We camped not far from a gathering of prospectors—hard looking men with canvas pants, floppy hats, each with a pick, shovel and pan never far out of reach. It seemed there wasn't a rock in the stream or its smaller tributaries that wasn't overturned. The gravel was shoveled into rockers, some of which were fed water by diversion dams upstream, feeding sluices bringing wash water to the devices.

As I set up a picket line after watering the stock, a gent with a belly the size of a large nail keg, buttons straining, and a black bushy beard with a head of hair to match, wandered over my way. Neither had been trimmed in a month of Sundays and looked as if they hadn't been exposed to a bar of soap in all that time. He was leading a skunk-striped donkey with a canvas-covered pack nearly as large as the animal.

He tied the donkey's lead to a sapling.

I had to laugh as the donkey tried to bite old beer belly, but he saw it coming and slapped the animal away. The donkey heehawed, spun and lashed out with both hind feet. But the man had wisely moved out of range.

I laughed. The man didn't appreciate it and gave me a hard look, then it softened as if he saw the humor in it.

"Howdy," he called out as he walked closer. He politely tipped his hat. Seemingly a change in attitude.

"Yes, sir," I replied.

"You the boss man?" he asked, but had a smug twinkle in his eye, and I knew he thought, by my youth, that I couldn't be.

"No, sir, that would be Mister Stadt, down there scrubbing up at the stream."

"You fellas got lots of stock for just the three of y'all."

"Mules for our trade goods, horses as we've come a far piece and lost a couple of partners along the way."

"Injuns?"

"Yes, sir."

"Well, from here on you should be shed of the savage. Modocs are off up north and the Miwok and others are peaceful. What's left of 'em after the pox got most."

"How's the prospecting coming?" I asked.

And like all prospectors, he replied with a shrug. None

of them ever want to let on they have a pouch full of gold. "Ain't enough to buy a pound of misery. However," his tone lightened, "I sure do fancy that tall black. Gelding, I'd guess."

"You'd guess right. But he's mine and he ain't for sale."

"I got five ounces of good pure dust you can trade for eighty dollars first assayer office you come to. That's a lot of money, young man. More than I bet you ever saw."

"That's true. Thanks, but no thanks."

"What y'all got in them packs. Looks like you're down to less than half a pack full, but I was up the hill aways watching you unload, and they sure looked to be heavy."

I studied him for a moment, a little suspicious about his interest. "Lead, bullet lead. You need to resupply?"

He shook his head. "I got plenty. Gold weighs like lead. Don't suppose you fellas played out some creek back aways and are heading for the assayers. My compliments should you be."

"We've come all the way from up in Oregon and wouldn't know a gold pan from a piss pot, so, no. It's bullet lead we're trading. Heard they were short in California."

He nodded, gave me a sour look, tipped his hat again, moved back and untied his now docile animal, then pulled his donkey on down to where Stadt was finishing his ablutions.

As I lined out the horses on one picket line and the mules another, then finished to wander down and wash up myself as Chang was about to call us to supper, the gent with the belly passed again and again tipped his hat.

I stopped and watched him as he was heading for the horses and not the way he'd come from.

He walked right to my black, the horse Tennison had bequeathed me, and threw a lead rope over his neck.

"Hey, what the devil are you doing?" I yelled and

stomped his way.

"Bought this horse and that black saddle from the man said he was captain of this outfit."

"No, sir, you didn't. I suggest you wander back to Mister Stadt and get your money refunded."

The man turned to face me at ten feet and rested his hand on the revolver he wore. "Look, sonny, I just bought him and if you don't like it, I suggest you take it up with that man I just paid."

I guess I was a bit quicker than old beer belly and before he could blink, had my Colt pulled, leveled, and cocked. "Get your hands off my horse and go get your refund. Buying a horse from a man who doesn't own it could get a fella hurt bad by the fella does own it."

"He said…"

"I don't give a tinker's damn what he said. You best worry about the fella whose finger is straining on this trigger."

I could hear footfalls behind me, running, and glanced over my shoulder to see Stadt puffing up the rise, then he yelled, "Zane, holster that weapon. You can have that gray. I sold…"

"The hell you did." I could feel my face going red and hot. "You can only sell what's your'n."

"I'm the captain of this outfit."

"No argument there. We've been forty days on the trail. You pay me eighty dollars and I'll go on my way, with my horses and my goods."

"You signed on to San Francisco. You can quit right now, but you ain't gettin' a dollar you do."

Chang had laid down his spoon and moved up behind Stadt, who glanced back at him, then turned back to me.

Then Stadt turned to beer belly. "How about you taking the gray instead?"

"The gray ain't half the animal the black is. No, sir, I bought the black and I'm taking him."

"Mister, you likely won't be able to take him to Hell with you, cause that's where you're headed you don't get that rope off my horse," I said it with finality, my eyes narrowing and my grip tightening on the Colt.

"Bull shit, you ain't got the sand..."

He jumped four feet straight back when I fired, and the dirt and rocks kicked up between his boots. He now stood, his eyes wide and round as the tin plates we ate out of, his palms extended in front of him. He looked as if he didn't know whether to run or piss his pants.

My voice was quiet and steady, his hands were shaking, my Colt steady. "I suggest you request your dust back from Stadt, then go on about your business."

He collected himself, then walked over and extended his hand out, palm up, to Stadt. Gunter Stadt eyed me like he'd like to pull his own Colt and belly shoot me, but as mine was loosely pointed his way, following the fat man there, he wisely pulled a small leather poke out of his pocket and handed it over.

"Sorry, but the boy is a little touched in the head and would likely shoot you down and try for me."

The man merely nodded and pocketed the pouch, then spun on his heel and led his donkey downstream. But he stopped, turned back and yelled at me, "You're bound for Hell yourself, you mouthy little whelp. You ain't seen the last of this."

I merely shrugged.

Stadt growled at me. "You're gettin' way above your station, boy. Don't you ever point that weapon even close to at me, or I'll shove it where the sun don't shine."

"I hear you, Mister Stadt. But then, I'll presume you'll never give me reason to point it at you? That said, you gonna stand by our agreement? Two dollars the day plus a one-hundred-dollar bonus we get safe to San Francisco?"

He stared at me for a long moment, then nodded his head. "That was the agreement and Gunter Stadt always honors his agreements." Then he turned and headed for Chang's fire and supper.

But I couldn't help but wonder. I'd begun to believe Mr. Gunter Stadt was not a man of his word.

As we ate, Stadt began to talk about Illinois, laughing and joking, his family, where he was born, as if nothing had happened between us.

I was even less comfortable with the man.

If I couldn't ride behind him, I decided to make sure Chang was between us. I sure as heck don't want him at my back, no matter how he talked fondly of family and home.

17

This is beautiful country, the northern end of the Sierra Mountains. I've heard that the highest mountain in all the states and territories is farther south in the Sierras. I'd like to see that, but more than that, I'd like to get to San Francisco, collect my money, and catch a ship up the coast to Oregon and Portland City, then a riverboat up the Columbia, the Snake, and jump off only a few miles from home. I'm damn sure lonely, with Chang hard to talk to with the language barrier and Stadt not fit to talk with. But, with luck, in a couple of weeks, I'll be heading north with only chores aboard a vessel of some sort. If what I hear is right, getting hired on a sailing vessel should be no hill for a stepper, as sailors from near a thousand sailing ships are now Argonauts, gold seekers, riding sluice rockers rather than the rocking deck of an ocean-going ship.

It seems we've passed the summit of this pass as we're mostly heading downhill, and occasionally ahead, I can see grass-covered hills as opposed to tree-covered. We were in a short uphill stretch, now moving away from the river and its gaggle of miners. It was a rocky rise with steep slopes on either side, a trickle of water snaked down the center of our tight trail. I was in the lead, dragging five mules, Chang behind me pulling four, our now three saddled-but-unridden horses were trotting free between Chang's string and Stadt. Stadt, as usual, was playing overseer and doing as little real work as possible.

I admit I was bored and paying little attention and was surprised when a voice rang out from only thirty or so feet up the slope.

"Pull your weapons with two fingers and drop them the trail, and we won't shoot y'all to hamburger."

I reined up and glanced up to my left to see the beer belly man holding a long gun, aimed at my midsection, and he couldn't miss at this short range. I extended my hands so he'd know I was no threat and looked back over my shoulder. Three more rough looking fellas rose up out of the rocks and brush. They were no more handsome than black beard, but just as well armed and had both Chang and Stadt covered.

"Yep," the fat man said, "you got enough lead pointed your way to cut you all in half a'fore you can reach. So, don't. Drop them weapons, easy like."

I had taken to keeping the Derringer Tennison had given me in my boot, and now was glad I had done so. I two-fingered the Colt out of its holster and flipped it into the soft dirt on my left side, the side where I'd dismount. If he hadn't shot me.

"Now that new Sharps of mine," he said, then guffawed. When he stopped laughing, he yelled back at Chang and Stadt. "You too, my boys get real impatient and might go to blastin'."

He laughed again, as I two-fingered the heavy Sharps out of my saddle scabbard and dropped it alongside the Colt.

"And the coach gun," he said. I had scabbards on either side of Sandy's saddle and holding the scattergun far toward the butt, slipped it out, and it joined the Colt and Sharps.

Then beer belly snapped, "Now, y'all get the hell off my new horses."

As he couldn't see my right hand, and the two on the right side of the trail were well back down the trail, covering Chang and Stadt, I slipped my hand in my right boot and fished out the Derringer. Hiding it in my palm, I threw a leg over Sandy's rump and slipped to the ground, watching for my chance.

The beer belly man started slipping down the bank to come even with us on the trail, stumbled and foolishly put the butt of his rifle down to steady himself.

I'd never fired the Derringer and said a silent prayer that it was functional and true. I raised and cocked it in the same motion.

He heard the ratchet and his head snapped my way. He started to yell, and I feared I had missed when the heavy little weapon kicked so hard it was pointing at the sky.

But his hand went to his throat, over that bushy black beard, and I realized the fifteen feet between us didn't impair my aim. Blood gushed between his fingers as he fell backwards onto the rock. He was trying to stand and raise his rifle, but the report of the belly gun was so near Sandy's ears he bolted forward and shouldered the big man sending him flying.

Hoping he was out of the fight; I dove for my rifle and long guns and came up with the Sharps. Cocking it as I raised it, I fired at a red-headed fellow who was trying to get a bead on me. But it was tough, as my mule string had also taken umbrage at the noise and all hell had broken loose on the trail. Mules were trying to run opposite ways up the banks or turn back, and it was a tangle of packs and humping backs and flying hooves as they fought against each other. I guess I missed with the Sharps but wasn't the only one who did as the reports of gunfire were so constant as to seem a continuous roar.

Chang traded shots with the same redhead I'd fired at, and both he and the man went down. Then he emptied his Colt at the next robber in line who was watching the fourth one run after Stadt. There was another man on the left side of the trail, and he was trying to clamber up on a rock pile to get a shot at me.

The left barrel of the scattergun, fired from the waist without aiming, discouraged him by taking half his head away.

Two shots rang out from fifty feet behind me and now it was my turn to try to get some height so I could see back down the trail. The fourth robber was hotfooting it back down the trail following Stadt who was obviously trying to get the hell away from the gunfight. But his horse was not attuned to gunfire in such close quarters and was doing a stiff-legged dance trying to shed himself of the tall thin man who called himself our captain.

Stadt was no cowhand. His arms were flopping around as he was trying to stay aboard and hang onto the long muzzle loader he used.

The robber was catching up and was over a hundred paces from me, too far for me to be confident that the scatter gun would do little more than sting him. My linsey-woolsey shirt had two pockets. I'd taken up the habit of carrying two paper cartridges in each pocket, and now was glad I had done so as my possibles bag was disappearing up the trail with my mount.

I snatched up the Sharps, opened the breech, fed in a fresh one and snapped the rifle to my shoulder. But I was a second too late. The fourth robber had caught up enough to be in range and was fanning shots from a revolver into Stadt's back. His horse settled into a run and Stadt lasted four or five jumps before slipping out of the saddle.

The robber holstered his weapon and turned back as if waiting to get a hoorah from the fat man. Rather he got a .52 caliber in the brisket, which blew him to his back, unmoving.

It suddenly got very quiet, as the mules had scrambled up the bank on both sides; our horses had galloped away. I could hear wheezing and blowing behind me and guess old beer belly was blowing and sucking wind through the hole in his throat. Then I heard cussing in a language I didn't understand but knew its source. Chang. At least he wasn't dead.

But I could see he was flat on his back, rolling back and forth as if in pain.

Dang if I wasn't the only man left standing.

18

While I stood staring at the bloody scene, waiting for the shivers to stop, I had to shake my head. Had I started all this gore and mayhem? Maybe I was wrong in not merely climbing down and handing over my horse and the goods—the gold—we were transporting. I could hear Chang still yelling his pain and displeasure, and see Stadt on his face in the rocks and dirt. Then I think on my pa, now three years passed, buried back on the Oregon Trail, who often told me a man had to stand up for himself and what was his—no matter the cost.

And this time the cost was dear.

I moved back down to the trail and hurried back to where Chang lay, his left hand pressed tightly to his right shoulder, blood oozing between his fingers. His eyes were clamped shut with the pain.

"Chang," I said, trying to keep my voice even although I still had the shakes, "It's all over. I need to dress that wound."

His eyes opened. "Broke shoulder. Got bone. Robbers?"

"All dead. Stadt too. We got a hell of a mess, and it

looks like it's up to me to clean it up. Be right back."

There was no doubt about the man whose head I'd blown half off, or the one Chang traded shots with as he was hit right under his left eye in an upward direction. He was dead before he hit the ground. I moved on down the trail, giving the two robbers that way a kick to make sure they were cold. Neither flinched. Stadt lay on his face, two holes in his back, neither weeping blood so there was no question his heart no longer pumped.

Nothing to be done for any of them, so I returned to Chang.

He said nothing, only lay with his hand pressed hard against the shoulder, his jaw clamped, his eyes pressed shut.

I peeled off my last shirt, pulled my hunting knife and cut it into strips. Chang's wound was three inches inside his shoulder just over his underarm, and an entry wound only. That meant the ball was still inside and would have to be extracted. I wondered how far we were from Leodocia and if there was a doc there—a surgeon with any luck at all. I stuffed the hole and quelled the bleeding. There was no question in my mind that bones were broken, probably his collar bone if nothing else. It was clear he'd be no help reloading and if he lived, his arm may be impaired for the rest of his days. I made him a sling to keep his arm from moving and managed to get him raised enough to get it on.

Then I stood and gazed around. Two packs with panniers lay in the trail. Up the slope stood two mules, their packs turned around and hanging beneath them. They glowered at me wondering why I wasn't up there putting things right. Down the trail a hundred and fifty paces, Sandy, my horse, Chang's gray, and Stadt's sorrel grazed as if all was right in the world, and beyond them two mules, shy of their packs, grazed quietly. Another grazed nearby, his pack and paniers hanging half off clumsily.

And far beyond them grazed the two horses that had been running free and following.

Dang if I didn't know where to start.

I fetched a water bag off one of the packs and returned to Chang. His eyes were open, and he was trying to sit up.

"Stay down, Mister Chang. You need to lie quiet for a while. We don't want that hole to go to bleedin' again. I got to collect goods and repack."

"We go on?" Chang asked.

"We go on to San Francisco and deliver the goods."

He merely nodded and lay back.

I found our little shovel and moved back to Stadt. I relieved him of his sidearm and gun belt, the little notebook he kept and its leather bag, and the contents of his pockets. I put his personal items in the leather pouch, including over two hundred dollars in gold eagles, and began digging his grave. It was hard going in the rocky soil and on a side hill. It was three feet deep and decided it was enough and eyeing him thinking it was gonna be a job to drag him up the slope, when a voice rang out.

It startled me and I jumped.

"Didn't mean to rattle you, youngster. What the hell happened here?"

I'd been working so hard I hadn't heard the stranger ride up. He was sitting a gray mule and dragging another black one packed with panniers and miner's implements.

"Robbers came at us in this narrow spot. Had us a little battle."

"I'd guess so," the man said. He had a revolver in hand but re-holstered it and dismounted. He walked over and stuck a hand out. "Oscar Peabody." And I shook.

"I'm Jake Zane. What's that accent, sir? I don't be-lieve…"

"Here all the way from Australia, mate. Come to join the diggings."

"I could use some help here. You oblige me and you could earn that gray horse grazing down there aways."

"Damned if I couldn't use another animal. But that's not necessary. One traveler should help another just to earn God's good grace."

"Well, sir, God's grace and a gray horse for you, should you pitch in."

"Let me care for my stock, mate, then we'll get at it. Dark is coming on afore we can near finish. There's a flat spot I passed back aways, and this little stream of water comes from a spring in the side hill. Good clean water there. Let's get camp set up there and this Chinee man settled down, the stock gathered up, and things squared away before we hoe this row of hard work."

"Makes sense," I say.

He helped me drag Stadt to the grave and just before we lay him to rest, suggested, "That's a decent shirt this cobber wears and it seems you're bare chested."

I nodded and we pulled his shirt off and even though bloodied front and back and with two holes amidst the blood both fore and aft, it was better than no shirt at all. I'd scrub it with lye soap when things settled down. I placed his wide-brimmed hat over his face as it bothered me to fling dirt in any man's face, no matter my disregard for him.

I led Sandy, the gray, and one of the mules a couple of hundred yards up the way we'd been headed to find the flat Oscar recommended and found it a fine camp site, just off the trail. Graze and clean water pooled below a spring in lichen-covered hard rock. I laid out some tarps and made a tent out of two of the ten by tens—pack covers—in a fashion pa called a hunter's tent. The country was what looked to be the last of the pines before we descended into the valley below. Just up the mountain were some stately ponderosas with their puzzle bark, but flanking the trail were aspens. Lucky. As cutting some saplings provided me with tent poles.

I was able to get Chang's good arm over my shoulder and after forty minutes of limping, resting, and lots of gritting teeth, got him under the cover of the tent.

Then it's line up the four bodies of the robbers well off the trail and fling a few shovelfuls of dirt over them—more than they deserve—collect the packs and their valuable 'loaves', and round up the rest of our critters. I did snatch another fine shirt off'n one of them. I collected eleven firearms from the four robbers and all the accoutrements including two folding knives and a revolving Colt's long arm I'd never seen the like of before.

Tomorrow, after I get our string back together, I'll hunt down their camp, or at least wherever they secured their stock.

I had more guns than a platoon of dragoons could use, so I gave Oscar a pair of Aston cap and balls—still in fine shape—and a new Navy Colt anyone would covet.

When Stadt talked about his birthplace in Cairo, Illinois, he mentioned a spinster sister, Ingrid. I know of no kin of Tennison, Alabama, or Jasper, but may find something of them when I reach San Francisco. I do know that Lord Willard Stanley-Smyth is to be waiting there. And if he's a fair man, he'll allow me to sell all that's left, and try and divvy it among myself and heirs. He'll have no claim to what I've been willed by Jasper, Alabama and Tennison or recovered from the four dead louts, so at least there will be that.

After all, if I get there, he'll be in receipt of many pounds of gold—or maybe I should say loaves.

Looks like it's all up to me now.

All I have to do is get there, another two hundred fifty miles or so full of miners and those catering to them—most of them honest.

Then there's the rest of 'em.

One thing's for sure, there's four less of 'the rest of them' now.

19

It was plain to me that Oscar Peabody knew all those loaves were not bullet lead. But he never attempted to open one nor did he question me beyond that simple explanation.

As I feared trying to train out more than five mules, he helped me reload all we could carry on the five—eighty pounds of loaves each in addition to our camp gear—and was more than pleased when I gifted him two mules and the gray. As Stadt's sorrel seemed the strongest and yet the most steady of our riding horses, I saddled him with Tennison's excellent black saddle, rigged a pack on the animal's back so Chang would have a sort of backrest, and left my Celestial friend, with a scattergun across his thighs, to guard over the string—and Oscar Peabody—while I backtracked the four robbers up and over the top of the pass until I found three animals and a broken lead rope where the fourth had pulled free. It was a sparse camp and other than a pair of fine canvas saddlebags packed with personals, I left it as is. I did free the three crow-bait horses and, after some consideration, the donkey. Consideration because I liked that donkey, he'd tried to both bite and kick ol' beer belly.

I offered Oscar Peabody a job, now that I seemed to be captain of the outfit. He refused me, even after I promised him three dollars a day for the near fifteen days it would take to reach San Francisco. He was adamant he'd find his own motherlode on up the trail somewhere and we parted with a handshake.

As we moved on down the trail, I was happy to note it was an easy downhill open trail. The hills were now chaparral covered, a few scrub oaks, but easy country. We made near twenty miles and I feared I'd killed Chang as I pulled him out of the saddle. It was a job unloading the mule train, making a rope corral, setting up a hunter's tent—the moon disappeared into an overcast shortly after rising and there were no stars to be seen—and cooking up the last of our bacon for me and a broth of jerky and some watercress for Chang.

He hadn't spoken a word since I'd loaded him aboard the sorrel early in the morning and didn't until I made him lie back in the tent on his bedroll and covered him with another pack tarp.

"Hard day," he said, his voice weak.

"Damn hard for you. But then you're a hard man, friend. I pushed it as we need to find a doc for that shoulder."

"Find Chineeman doc in San Francisco."

"Maybe, surely, but we gotta to get that ball out. Leodocia, first. Easy riding now, we'll make it tomorrow."

"If Chang still alive."

"You gotta stay alive, Mister Chang. You're the only friend I got left."

"You say I strong. I stay strong."

"Good, Leodocia, then your Chineeman can give you all the snake oil you can handle."

It was a good thing I rose early. It had rained in the night and our camp was a muddy mess. It took me an hour and a half to cook us some grub and load the train.

I hadn't corralled the two horses that I'd left to trail us, and they'd wandered off in the night. They weren't necessary for our quest, so I didn't bother to hunt them. It seemed far too important to get Chang to a healer.

So, we set out at a quick pace. I made Chang take the lead so I wasn't constantly having to turn back to make sure he was still with us. Chang again was silent, never complaining, though I know the jerking pace of being on horseback had to be excruciating. We passed at least six groups of Argonauts as we neared Leodocia and I yelled out to each, "You got a doctor?" but got nothing but head-shakes.

The sorrel wanted to move at a slow walk as Chang was hanging his head and not gigging him along, so I loosened Sandy's lead rope and occasionally popped the sorrel on the butt to move him along.

The sun was just kissing the horizon and low mountains to the west, a streak of blood red sky under the overcast followed, when I saw the lights of Leodocia ahead.

I yelled at Chang. "Stay strong, Mister Chang. Town ahead and a soft bed for you."

He gave me a wave with his good hand, and it pleased me he was able.

I was happy that I'd pocketed those twenty ten-dollar gold pieces of Stadt's as we came to the Sacramento river. The only building on our side was the ferry house, and the ferryman was quick to inform me that it would be two dollars for my five mules and our two horses and two men to cross.

I was in no mood to argue, so paid up.

As we clomped in on the mud street, I had little hope

of a real doctor. The town was a general store, a livery, a barber shop and dentist, bank, Wells Fargo office and assayer, four saloons, a hotel, an opera house, and, beyond, spotted cabins and houses.

I rode straight to the two-story hotel, reined up in front, and dragged my worn-out body in. I was bone tired, not so much from the ride but from the worry.

A thick-lensed bespectacled fellow in a striped shirt with garters on the arms holding his sleeves up off his hands eyeballed me with a frown. He waited as I shuffled to the counter, his hands flat.

"Long ride?" he asked.

"Too dang long. I got a hurt man outside and we need a room and a doctor."

"This ain't no hospital, but so long as he ain't got the smallpox or some such."

"Gunshot to the shoulder. Bandits back up the trail more'n a day."

"The devil you say. Should I get the sheriff. We got one."

"No, sir. Just a room so I can get him horizontal."

"Two dollars a day includes coffee in the morning. Bath is out back with hot water in the kettle over the fire, another quarter dollar you should want to partake."

I took a deep breath. I'd never stayed in a hotel so had no idea how expensive it was.

"And a doctor?" I asked, fishing in my pocket for the eight dollars in change I got after paying for the ferry.

"No full-fledged doc but we got a nurse lady who has a fine hand."

"If that's it. He's got a ball in his shoulder needs diggin' out."

"Robert!" he yelled over his shoulder, and a boy of ten or so appeared in a door behind the desk.

"Yes, Pa."

"Go fetch the widow O'Farrel and tell her bring her instruments."

"You bet, Pa."

I yelled after him. "I got mules and horses out there, loaded with my goods. Four bits you keep an eye on them soon as you get back. I'll be a while."

"You bet I will. I'll watch 'em all night for four bits."

And he hotfooted it out into the dark street.

"I'll need a hand unloading my friend." I dropped a silver dollar coin on the desk.

I spun on my heel and headed out with the desk clerk on my heels. He followed me up beside the sorrel, then stopped short.

"He's a Chinaman," the clerk observed.

"Never said he wasn't," I said, and glanced back at him and saw he was backing away.

"You never said he was."

"So, what? Don't change the fact he's shot."

"We don't house Chinamen, Mexicans, Negroes or Indians."

"He'll be in our room. No one will see he ain't lily white like you and me."

"We don't house…"

"I heard you and I appreciate you making an exception for my hurt friend."

"Can't do it," he said, and backed farther away. Then he yelled, "Robert, hold up."

I was too tired to argue, so I just pulled my Colt and stuck it under the desk clerk's chin. "I got one more dollar for a room for tonight. That's three damn dollars and highway robbery at that, but it's cheaper than me wasting a ball and powder blowing your damn head off then paying some attorney to explain you're a damn welcher."

The boy hadn't answered, so I guess he was still after the widow O'Farrel.

I could hear the air whistle into the clerk's lungs as the cold barrel of the Colt pushed his chin up.

"We got us a deal?" I asked.

"You bet," he mumbled. I holstered the Colt and he helped me dismount Chang. With his good arm over the clerk's shoulder and me helping from behind, we got him up the three steps to the boardwalk and inside. Then it was down the hall on the lower floor and he used a skeleton key to open the last room before a door that led outside to the privy. "Keep him out of sight. I'll send the widow back."

"Thank you," I said, in a tone quite different than the one I'd been using.

I got Chang peeled down to his long Johns and under the covers about the same time the door opened, without bothering with a knock. To my surprise, it was not the widow O'Farrel, but a man a half head taller than me with a handlebar mustache, pork chop sideburns and a big five-pointed copper badge.

20

"I'm Sheriff Albert Broder. Turn around and face the wall, young fella."

"Sir," I said. "My friend here…"

He drew fast enough to make me think he might be a gunfighter gone honest. I raised my hands so he'd know I was no threat.

He repeated, "Now, turn around a'fore I knock you looplegged."

"Yes, sir," I said, as I did a one eighty and he fished my Colt out of my holster.

"You assaulted John Rudin, the hotel clerk, with this firearm." It was a statement, not a question.

I sighed deeply. "To my way of thinking…"

"Don't give a hoot nor a holler about your way of thinkin'. Did you or did you not shove this under Rudin's chin?"

"Yes, but I'd already paid for the room and then he tried to refuse it to me, so you see, he's the one breaking the law here."

"Take to that chair over in the corner."

I did so, folding my hands in my lap like I was a

schoolmarm in church.

He continued. "How so Rudin broke the law?"

"I paid. He refused the goods. And I didn't have time to argue. My friend here is bad wounded and needed to be down and tended to."

Now it was the sheriff's turn to sigh. To my relief, he holstered his own big revolver. "Okay, young man," then he studied Chang for the first time, who was on his back, his head slightly elevated on the pillow, cutting his eyes from one of us to the other as he followed the conversation.

Sheriff Broder gave me a hard look. "This man's a Celestial?"

"He is."

"Didn't Rudin tell you the hotel doesn't cater to Celestials, Negroes, Mexicans or Indians."

"Yes, sir, he did, but after he'd accepted the money. My pa always told me when you accept the money, you've concluded the transaction and there's no going back."

Sheriff Broder actually smiled and nodded his head. "Your pa told you that, did he?"

And I nodded in return.

But his smile faded. "What's your name, young fella?"

"Zane. Jake Zane."

"Well, Jake Zane. Seems as if no one was hurt, so I'm gonna have Rudin return your money on your way out. No saloon in Leodocia, no hotel, no brothel, does business with Chinamen, Negroes, Mexicans or Indians. So, it was a mistake…"

"Out of the way, Albert," a lady's voice rang out and she not only said it but elbowed the sheriff aside. "I'm Prudence O'Farrel," she announced to Chang and me.

She carried a small black leather bag and opened it as she moved to Chang's side.

"He ain't stayin' here," Sheriff Broder snapped.

The lady was nearly as tall as me and heavier. Her gray hair was pulled tight and rolled in a bun on the back of her head. She spun on her heel and shoved a stiff index finger in the sheriff's chest. "I don't abide by your damn stupid laws, Albert. And the next time you or Molly get the croup or that big toe and your gout goes to paining you, don't bother coming begging."

"Prudence," he said, back peddling a little. "You see to him, then he has to find another place…."

"Horse apples. When he's well enough to do laundry, or work the tailings, all you highbinders will be happy to have him at work for pig's feet and slop. Now, go peddle your wares elsewhere and let me get to work. You go put the clerk's mind to rest."

"How do you propose I do that?"

"You're the law, lay down the law."

Sheriff Broder shook his head, seemingly resigned, if disgusted, and left the room. But he paused in the doorway, turned and gave me a hard look. "Mister Zane, you keep that iron tucked away or you'll find yourself lookin' through my flat iron bars."

"Yes, sir," I said to his back as he closed the door, then he stuck his head back in. "Y'all keep this door closed so the other guests don't see that heathen hereabouts."

I said, "Yes, sir," but Miss Prudence merely waved over her shoulder as if she was shooing a fly as she examined Chang's wound.

"Got to come out," she said, then turned to me. "Take that pitcher. Go get some clean towels and boiling water from the kitchen. If Rudin gives you any lip, tell him he's got to answer to me. His wife is gonna need a midwife soon and I'm it for many a mile."

When I returned, she was placing a rag over a bottle

mouth, but holding the substance at arm's length, then quickly re-stoppered it. Chang was shy his long Johns top and the pillow removed so he lay flat. She had the chimney off a coal oil lamp and the flame turned high.

"What the devil is that?" I demanded, as I sat the milk white pitcher of hot water and a stack of towels down.

"This is chloroform. The latest. I had to have it shipped all the way from San Francisco."

"What's it do?" I demanded.

"Puts you to sleep and you don't feel the pain. First used by a Scottish doctor, name of Simpson, brought over the Atlantic by Sam Guthrie and some others. Dang if it ain't a wonder. I sawed off a fella's leg, gone green it was, just below the knee…"

"Leg fine," Chang said with some trepidation and wide eyes.

"You bet it is," Miss Prudence said, reassuringly, and gave him a smile. "This little mining job is hardly worth the waste of good chloroform, but what the hay. You'll have that ball to hang on a string around your neck lickity split."

"What lickity split?" Chang asked.

"Lay your head flat and keep your hands at your side. This don't smell too sweet, but you've had things stink more."

And she jabbed the rag under his nose, careful to stay as far back as she could and still apply the soaked patch of cloth.

As soon as Chang's eyes closed, she reached to a cloth she'd spread out, now lined with instruments, picked up one with a narrow wood handle and a short blade, and moved the blade back and forth over the flame. Then to my surprise stuck Chang a poke near the wound. A drop of blood formed, but he didn't even flinch.

"Seems to work," I said.

"I may need some fresh chloroform before we're finished. You saw how I handled it, and you do the same, need be. Won't do to have my assistant sagging to the floor asleep before we're done."

"Yes, ma'am," I said.

I watched as she made a cut right across the wound, enlarging the opening to an inch or so. Again, Chang didn't flinch.

"Hand me those forceps?"

"Ma'am?"

"Looks like scissors but with teeth on the business end."

I knew exactly which she meant and handed them quickly. As she had with the knife, she passed the end over the flame, then drove it into the wound. She poked and prodded, then opened the ends inside and was trying to grasp something unseen, the ball, no doubt.

"Bejesus and hobbledehoy," she said as she worked.

"Ma'am?" I said, not understanding.

"I don't curse, young man. That's as close to a…" Then she turned and smiled, as she extracted the instrument, slathered in blood and muck, but tightly in the teeth of what she'd called forceps. She reached over and let the ball clatter in the white porcelain bowl I'd snatched the pitcher from.

She quickly fingered a needle and some thread from her kit, passed the needle over the flame, threaded it as quickly as any seamstress, and with six or eight stitches had Chang's wound pulled shut and barely weeping.

"He'll be fine," she said. "He'll wake soon. Might have a headache, but that's it. Keep the arm in that sling you made for at least a month. And don't let him move it. His collar bone is sure enough broke and won't heal if he moves it."

"Yes, ma'am," I said, giving her a wide smile. "He's strong and tough."

"You got any silver or gold?" she asked, and put a hand out, palm up.

"How much?" I asked, waiting to be hit with a still bill as I'd already come to knowing that everything in gold country California came dear.

"Dollar for my time and skill, and a dollar for the chloroform and thread."

"My pleasure," I said, expecting four times that amount. "How long before we can move him?"

"I'll tell Rudin you'll be out of here after lunch tomorrow. I've got a room at my place, a half dollar a day for each of you with the best cooking in town—out of town a smidgen, actually. Ask anyone the way there. Unless you'd rather room up at Sadie's brothel. She'll charge you at least ten dollars a day with the benefits they offer and the pox comes with the deal, no extra charge."

"We'll find our way to your place and thank you. At least I hope thank you. Should he wake up, thank you."

"He'll wake up. You come on out to my place. Or better yet, I'll send my girl to fetch you. Ju Ling. Does Chang speak Cantonese?"

I shrugged.

"No matter. They'll get along real well. She's a pretty little thing. Half the Celestials for miles around line the fences just to look at her while she's hanging clothes on the line."

She packed up and headed for the door and as she reached for the knob, someone beat on it. She opened it to see the clerk, Rubin. He was red in the face with his fists knotted at his sides.

"You got to stop with the noise," she snapped, and that

stiff finger poked him in the brisket.

"When can he leave?" Rudin asked, as he backpeddled.

"Six weeks, how's that?" she said.

"You'll get me fired, Prudence."

"He'll be gone after lunch tomorrow. Now get back to your books and leave these young men alone. They've had enough trouble for one day."

And she closed the door, just as Chang moaned.

21

I was worried sick about my cargo outside. But I guess all the gold on earth isn't worth a man's life, so I stood by another few minutes until Chang came around. I poured him a cup of water from the pitcher, now cool enough to drink.

When he finished his drink and seemed fully recovered, I brought him up to date. "Fifty caliber ball is out and in the bowl there should you want a souvenir. I've got to take care of our freight and animals. You stay in the room, use the chamber pot if necessary, as we're not welcome here. Get better as we gotta find a new place to roost by noon tomorrow. You gonna be all right?"

"Got headache but be fine."

"I'll be back." And I hurried out.

As promised, the boy was parked on the boardwalk watching the stock and packs. I passed him a half-dollar and got a big smile.

"The livery man a fair gent?" I asked.

"He's my uncle, and you bet he's a Christian man. Everyone calls Horace by his nickname, Bones. But everything is running proud prices around the diggings.

Yesterday they were getting fifty dollars the hundred pounds for flour."

"Well, seems your uncle is the only port in this storm. What time does the Wells Fargo office open?"

"Eight AM, like most everything. Sometimes earlier if there's a stage due to depart."

"Tell you what...you want to make another dollar?"

"Does a chicken peck?"

"Ask your pa if it's okay if you sleep in Chang's room tonight? I'll be sleeping with our supplies. If things are coming that proud, all this gear might be too tempting."

"Don't have to ask. Pa knows the worth of a dollar."

"Okay. Fetch my friend a bowl of soup." I handed him another dollar. "Then you camp out in the room. He starts having trouble or asks you to, you come fetch me faster than that chicken you mentioned can peck. Got it?"

"Yes, sir. Way faster."

The livery man, Robert's uncle, had gone home for the night but had empty stalls. I offloaded the packs in the tack room, put our two horses and five mules in stalls, found some grain and nosebags and feed, then lashed the door to where I'd stowed the packs tight with a line. It was the best I could do in the way of a lock. At least an intruder would have to work hard to gain access.

I climbed into the loft and rolled my bedroll in the loose hay.

In the middle of the night, I sat up quickly with a noise, and stared down and checked the tack room door, visually, and the rest of the livery. Nothing. Then a rat scampered so close to my stocking feet I damn near jumped out of my sox. I laughed at myself and went back to sleep.

A little light was peeking through the jambs of the second-floor loading door of the loft when I awoke. I climbed down, pleased to see my rope lashing of the tack room door was still in place. I messed with filling the water buckets in the stalls for my stock and others from a well in the back of the livery, then still having to kill time until the hostler showed up, mucked out the stalls, working around my stock and the others until I'd finished mucking the whole barn.

Finally, I heard someone enter the little office at one front corner of the barn, walked up and opened the pass-through door.

The man was already seated at his desk and stood quickly when I entered.

"Dang if you didn't startle me. You move quiet."

It was obvious why they called him Bones. He was my height and likely fifty pounds lighter. I was surprised he didn't rattle when he rose. Pa would have called him Mr. Spindleshanks.

"Sorry. Came in after you'd closed up. I owe you for the stabling."

"Let's see what you got," he said and led me out into the barn. "How many?" he asked.

"Seven total. Two to a stall, 'cept for the odd one, grained 'em all this morning."

He walked over and checked each stall. "Dang if you didn't muck them out."

"Yes, sir. All of them."

"How much grain?"

"Two inches in each nosebag."

"Well, sir, normally it would be two dollars the animal…"

I interrupted him. "I wasn't buying them from you, sir. I already own them."

He laughed. "Like I said, normally, it would be two dollars in this high-priced time we're in, but since you labored around the place, how about one dollar."

"Twice what I'd have to pay in Lewiston."

"Which Lewiston?"

"Oregon territory, on the Snake."

"You just come down?"

"Arrived here yesterday, straight away from there."

"I got a cousin there, last I heard of him. You know a fellow named Rupert?"

"Rupert Rudin. Dang. I didn't put the name together from the fellow runs the hotel. Your brother runs the hotel?"

"You bet. Rupert still in Lewiston?"

"Yes, sir. At least he was when I left, and, unless he sold the saddlery, he's still there."

We talked for another half hour. I filled him in on his cousin and was glad I did, when he dropped the price to six bits an animal.

Concerned, of course, about my goods, I asked, "Will my packs be safe until I can get Mister Chang settled and load up and get out of here?"

He laughed. "Tiny will be along shortly. As you might guess, Tiny is as big and as dumb as one of your mules. But someone try and take so much as a kernel of grain and Tiny will pound them into road apples."

I laughed. "Sounds just fine."

On the way back to the hotel, I passed a saloon that seemed to double as a café and grabbed a quick breakfast, for the obscene price of a dollar for coffee, two fried eggs, and potatoes. It would have been another dollar had I added a slice of ham or a couple of slices of bacon. Before I left, I got a fried egg between a couple slices of toasted bread to take to Chang.

When I walked into the hotel, the insulting clerk was behind the desk.

He didn't bother with hello. "When are you getting

that heathen out of here?"

"And good morning to you, sir. I'm sure the sheriff informed you we'd be leaving just after noon."

"He did, and ten AM is our check out time, so you'll owe me another..."

"Mister Rudin. Dang if you ain't an insulting..." I started to say son of a bitch but contained myself. "If you ain't looking for another go-round with me. If Mister Chang is up to it, we'll be out when the sheriff said we should be out. Call him over here and we'll discuss..."

"Be out by one o'clock and there'll be no charge."

"If not, I'll pay for another night and we'll hang around."

"No, sir, you'll be out."

I waved over my shoulder as I headed back to the room. When I entered, I was pleased to see Robert perched on the edge of the bed, jawing with Chang. I handed him a dollar and got a big smile.

"I was getting hungry. I brung some coffee to Mister Chang, but I don't drink the brew."

"Thank you. Tell your daddy I think he should take a lesson from your good heart."

He laughed. "You tell him. I don't believe it's my place." And he hurried out to find his breakfast, I'd guess.

I handed Chang his food. "Ain't much, but it'll have to do for a while."

"Look fine," he said and started chomping, holding it with one hand as his other was in a sling.

I'd been thinking on my situation, and what I had to do. I decided I couldn't be hindered by a wounded man, no matter how I respected and valued him.

As he finished, I asked, "Can you make it a half mile or so to some new facilities?"

"Can do," he said, and I got him to his feet, unsteadily, but to his feet. I immediately knew we wouldn't be walking a half-mile.

22

As it happened, Chang was still too dizzy to make it far at all. Rather than try the half mile to the Prudence O'Farrel place, I helped him to the livery and requested the rental of a buggy or wagon.

Bones took one look at Chang and said, "I was riding out that way to see if I could buy a few sacks of grain. Help me harness the buggy and I'll give y'all a ride. No charge, if'n you take a letter to Rupert for me."

"Pleased. Likely be a month or more to get it there."

"Or two months should I try the mail. Faster if you carry. Let's harness up."

"Is your man here?" I asked, then had the questioned answer as we walked out into the barn. Tiny was among the biggest men I've ever seen and looked as if he could pick a mule up under each arm. He gave me a nod, and I nodded back.

I had parked Chang in the office chair, and we harnessed a piebald mare to Mr. Bones' buggy and then loaded Chang in the left seat. I climbed into a little flat baggage area behind the seats, and we were off.

I hadn't seen a whitewashed house since we left Missouri, and a two-story one at that, with robin blue trim and painted shutters. And outbuildings: a privy, barn, and what looked to be a bunkhouse.

I realized it was mid-June and getting hot, as Prudence had flowers blooming in window boxes and lining a whitewashed picket fence.

A pretty young Celestial girl ran from the front door as Bones pulled rein.

"I was coming to fetch you," she said, as we got Chang down. We did not climb the steps to the house, rather moved around the house to the building that looked to be bunkhouse or guest quarters and entered to find a small parlor and four rooms off a short hallway.

"Missus O'Farrel runs a boarding house?" I asked.

"She does. I will care for Mister Chang. Please, you come in before you leave."

"Yes, ma'am," I said.

Then as I sat Chang on the bed, she started to unbutton his shirt.

"No, I do," he said.

I smiled as he seemed a bit shy.

"You do," she said. "I will return with fresh dressing for your wound."

He nodded. While she was gone, I dug some gold coins from my pocket.

"I can't stay until you're well," I said. "I hired on to deliver the goods, and I'll do as I agreed, or my pa would return from the grave and take a razor strap to my behind." He gave me a smile, then a worried look, but looked relieved when I handed him ten ten-dollar gold pieces.

"When I settle up with this John Bull, I'll send you a draft via Wells Fargo for what more you got coming. You ever want to come up Oregon way, I'll find a place for you."

"John Bull?"

"The Englishman. This Lord Willard Stanley-Smyth is supposed to be waiting for his goods at the Niantic Hotel in San Francisco."

He nodded, sad eyed, but no sadder than I felt.

"I hate like the devil to leave you," I said, not only because he was a friend, but also because I'd now be on two hundred or so miles of trail alone with four hundred pounds of gold loaded onto six mules. I don't know of any man who'd relish that task.

I shook hands with him, and reluctantly left. I conferred with Prudence O'Farrel, assuring her Chang could pay his keep, and shared a cup of tea in her parlor before I set out on foot back to the livery. She pleased me by saying she'd care for him, even if he couldn't pay. A true Christian woman.

Now, did I really want to try this next two hundred miles on my own, dragging five mules, watching for bandits, sleeping without a guard?

Bones was back in his office when I returned, so I asked him, "Any honest man around I might hire to accompany me to San Francisco?"

He laughed and shook his head. "Every able-bodied man I know is in the diggings. Afore this gold came along, they'd beat down the door to get a dollar a day—not now."

I guess big Tiny overheard my question and stuck his head in the door. "I'm wantin' to get back to San Fran and catch me a ship to Los Angeles and see me ma. You gonna pay?"

"Been paying two dollars a day," I said.

Bones rose from behind his desk. "Hey, hold on. I need Tiny here."

Tiny would have none of it. "Mister Bones, I done tolt you I was headin' home come summer. I'm headin' home."

"Dang, Tiny," Bones moaned, "it's barely summertime."

"Yes, sir, but ain't 'barely' same as 'is'?" He looked questioningly at Bones, as if he wasn't sure.

So, I stepped in. "Mister Tiny, this is not only a packing job, but with things like they are, it's a guard job as well. Can you handle a firearm?"

"Been huntin' rabbits and squirrels since I was waist high."

"Yes, sir, but rabbits and squirrels are not a man with a firearm pointed at you, and that's what robbers are prone to do. It's two dollars a day and found, such as it is at the campfire."

"Don't know from prone, but if'n a fella is pointin' a gun at you don't it mean he wants to do hurt to you?"

"I'd guess it does."

"My ma and my pa said don't never let no one do hurt to you, so I guess if'n I can hit a rabbit on the run or a rodent high in a pine I could hit a big ol' robber."

"You'll have a coach gun on your person so if he's inside of sixty feet or so, you'll hit him if'n you aim his direction." So, I turned to Bones. "You got a big old draft horse out there. Does he ride?"

"He does. Rides, plows, pulls ore wagons," Bones said, but I could tell he was irritated.

"So, what's he worth?"

"Twenty-five dollars. He'll pack two hundred pounds or more."

"Yeah, but will he ride three hundred?" I said, glancing at Tiny and guessing his weight.

"He's what Tiny rides when he goes on errands."

"Then since you've done me good turns, here's the deal. I'll give you twenty-five dollars for the plow horse and you throw in a saddle that fits him and Tiny, and I'll throw in that tall sorrel Mister Chang was riding and the sorrel's gear."

He looked a little surprised, even for the horse trader I knew him to be, as every livery man was.

He shrugged and asked, "What's wrong with the sorrel. That's a fifty-dollar horse if he's a dime."

"He is, but like I say, you did me a good turn and I'm leaving you without a swamper."

He hesitated for a moment, then walked out and to the sorrel's stall. He checked his teeth and rubbed down every leg looking for flaws, then eyed me. "Dang if he don't seem sound."

"Sound as a twenty-dollar Liberty gold piece."

He shakes his head again, but steps forward and sticks out a hand. "Hell's fire, Tiny's likely gonna leave nonetheless. You got a deal."

"My pa told me the only good deal was when it was a good deal for both sides. So, you happy?"

"As a toad next to a road apple buzzing with flies," he said, and we shook.

I turned to Tiny. "Mister Tiny, fetch your personals, your travel gear and saddle that horse while I get this string strung out."

"Sorry to see you go, Tiny," Bones said. "I owe you three days." And he headed for his office.

We're getting a late start, but it's easy foothill and valley travelling with plenty of water, if we're to follow the Sacramento River, and, so I'm told, it goes where we're going, all the way to San Francisco bay.

I have seventy-five dollars in gold and silver, but God willing, that's more than I'll need. Then I laugh at myself remembering I've got four hundred pounds of gold at sixteen dollars an ounce. Guess I won't run out of money on the way, should I have to dip into the boss's plentiful reserves.

As we head out, I stop at the mercantile and invest in five pounds of beans, a side of bacon, coffee, and some hardtack. As I leave, I find it hard to believe I'm near twenty-five dollars lighter than when I shoved through the door.

But at least we're on our way.

Now all I have to do is not pick up a belly full of lead.

23

I was fooling myself thinking this valley travelling easy. It's hot and we haven't gone a mile before I'm having to mop the sweat out of my eyes and am down to my long John tops. I'm leading three mules, and the lead string. My new employee, Tiny, follows with two. But the heat is not the only discomfort. There's not a single mosquito. All of them are married with plenty of relatives, and we've both slapped ourselves silly by the time we rein up for jerky and hardtack and blow the stock.

We've not only passed a half-dozen groups of hopeful miners, but at least that many flat boats working their way up stream. And they are covered, stem to stern, gunnel to gunnel, with Argonauts. I enjoy the sound of singing, banjos, fiddles, juice harps, and even one group with a pianoforte. As they pass, I wonder how many of them will be singing joyfully in a month?

We only make ten or twelve miles before the sun dips behind the mountains on the east side of the valley. It's a low range, half the size of those on the east. The country we've been crossing is mostly grassland, but the occasional wetland is swampy and hard going—belying again my thinking it would be easy valley riding. I'm occasionally impressed by a few spotted live oaks with massive trunks and lower limbs. It's not the crags and crannies in this valley that concerns but the mud and mosquitos. I guess we're destined to be tested all the way to the end of the first leg of my journey, Lewiston to San Francisco. Then, hopefully, an easy ride on ship and riverboat to home.

Bones gave me terse directions to the next spot of civilization, unless you considered the flood of Argonauts such. I didn't, as they were a rough-looking lot and seemingly single-minded—get to the diggings with little regard for long-time residents or even passersby.

It is only forty miles from Leodocia to Rancho del Arroyo Chico, an old Spanish land grant founded by an early settler, now known as General John Bidwell, then twice that distance to Sacramento City. Since we got a late start, it'll likely be two nights on the trail, dawn to dusk travel tomorrow, then this Arroyo place the middle of day three.

Tiny was a fine travelling companion, doing more than his share in packing and unpacking, cooking and swamping up afterward. And he travelled in silence, keeping his own counsel, which was fine with me.

We camped next to the river the first night, not far from where a flatboat had tied up. I guess the curves and sandbars of the Sacramento were too much in the dark.

We were invited to join the camp and partake in a card game, but neither of us were skilled and willing to risk what little we had. At least what little I had that was mine.

The mosquitos seemed less prevalent on the riverbanks, so I surmised it was occasional swampy areas they preferred. That gave me an idea. The river flat boats were not only going upstream full of folks and supplies but returning near or totally empty.

Come morning, while Tiny worked saddling and

packing, I tried to wave down the first two river boats to no avail. They merely waved at me as if my jumping up and down and trying to wave them from center stream to bank was the sign of a crazy man, not one willing to pay to come aboard.

We were well into the day when the first snake rose its ugly head. Four fellas, not riding, but dragging two donkeys and two small mules, stopped in the trail ahead, in a narrow spot. They said nothing as we approached, until I reined up not ten feet from them. The man in the lead was a barrel-chested lout with wild straw-colored hair, which under his wide brimmed hat was askew in every direction.

"You fellas taking root there?" I asked.

"Nope," the nearest one said, with a curl of his lip. Then he added, "fact is we been outta grub for the last two days."

"You're only a day and a half or so from Leodocia, and a fully stocked mercantile."

He gave me a sardonic smile. "Fact is, we're outta coin too. So, the price of passing is a few pounds of grub."

"So that's a toll road and you're the toll taker?"

"That's the way it looks, shoat."

I'm eyeballing him, wondering why I don't have my Colt palmed, when I glance back over my shoulder and to my surprise, don't see Tiny aboard his old draft horse.

Son of a gun done run off, I'm thinking as I turn back to the barrel-chested man blocking my trail.

"Friend," I said, trying not to intimidate him, "we've got just enough to get us where we're going and no more."

"Friend? You're calling me friend and you won't share a little grub. That's not friendly."

"We crossed a little stream a mile or so back and there were carp, some as long as my arm, heading up stream.

I'd guess they might be spawning. If I wasn't in a hurry, I'd have jumped off and caught a few with my hands. Why don't you…"

"What the hell you got in all them packs, it ain't grub?"

"Mining supplies. We been in the diggin's and are giving it up."

The man and his friends all laughed at that, and he said, "In the diggin's, so you got a poke full of gold?"

We both reached at the same time, but before I could pull my iron or he his, Tiny stepped out of the willows with a leap, had a hand on straw-hair's wrist, jerked him out of the saddle as if he was a skinny kid, and slammed him into the rough trail.

"What the…" a man behind him yelled, and reached for his sidearm, but I was already drawn and cocked.

"Don't pull it, pilgrim," I said, and he paused. Paused just long enough for Tiny to leap the two long strides and jerk that one from his mount, this time lifting him overhead before slamming him into the trail.

"Anybody else?" I yelled at the two following, but they replied by dragging their donkeys off the trail and into the willows as fast as they could pull. The first two were moaning as if they'd been run over by a beer wagon loaded with kegs. I believe the first boy, old straw hair, had a busted wing as he was holding it about bicep high with his off hand, and rolling back and forth moaning.

"I'll cover them two you want to mount back up," I said to Tiny, who was dusting his pants off.

He looked up at me. "These here two was pointing them guns at you. You want me to tear their heads off'n they shoulders?"

I tried to quell my smile, but it was hard to do. "No,

thank you, Tiny. I believe they are bad men, but not quite that bad. Sling their sidearms off into the brush and we'll just ride on."

He gathered up two cap and ball pistols and slung them. One, so far, I thought I heard it splash in the Sacramento on the far side of the willows.

Tiny shoved by and mounted the big old horse, and I gigged Sandy on by the two lying by the trail.

"Try them carp, back about a mile. They eat okay if you can work around the bones."

I couldn't help but laugh and compliment myself on my selection of employees.

When it came time to hunt a camp, I decided it was safer to pull off the trail a good way. No sense tempting fate by teasing hungry Argonauts with the smell of bacon and beans.

Tomorrow we should make Rancho del Arroyo Chico, and some whisper of civilization again. Then only two hard days to Sacramento City. With only the gold mine town of Ophir City twixt Chico and there. We'll pull away from the Sacramento River to stay near the foothills and out of the swampy territory, which means I won't be able to flag down a riverboat, but I haven't had any luck doing so as it seems they're all in too big a hurry to get down river to pick up another paying load of hopeful millionaires.

But things have been tame, so far, and Ophir City and surrounds are said to be the wild and woolly gold country at its best and sinful worst.

Had we been able to stay on the Feather River, we'd have come to Ophir City straight away, but were told the country rough and full of miners all the way down to a rough place called Bidwell Bar. Where the current owner of Rancho del Arroyo Chico had panned his fortune.

Up and down stream and in every drainage, miners now upended the countryside and streambeds. It was safer to avoid so many hungry gold seekers. I'd guess many would think it easier to pick a few hundred pounds off mule backs than grub and muck it from muddy shoals.

As much as I enjoy civilization, I believe it wise to fight shy until I have no choice.

24

Other than slappin' and scratchin', it was easy going to the hillside overlooking Rancho del Arroyo Chico. I'm a little surprised to see a town that is nowhere near what I'd heard. A general store, a hotel, a post office, and a flour mill. Not a saloon or brothel in sight. Someone was funnin' me when they described this place.

We rode in and tied up in front of the hotel, which also had a small sign saying Café. I'd seen Tiny destroy a bowl of beans and half-dozen slices of bacon. Even though I was sure I couldn't afford to fill him up, I offered.

"How about some fancy cooking?"

"I'd as soon save my hard earned so's to give some to my ma, should she still be in Los Angeles."

"My treat," I said, then cautioned, "so long as it's not princely prices."

He smiled and nodded. "Princely means like in the palace."

"Exactly. I heard a beefsteak in San Francisco could go as high as five dollars, so, if one serving doesn't fill you up, we still got some bacon and beans."

"Well," he said, glancing around, "this ain't San Francisco, so let's find out. And fair enough about following up with bacon and beans, need be."

We hitched the animals, loosened their cinches and strode in. A fine-looking gentleman in a cutaway coat and four-in-hand tie greeted us as we turned from the entry and guest registration into the café.

"Gentlemen," he said.

"Yes, sir," I answered, "we'd like to eat, should you have room." As there was only one other pair of fellows in the place, he knew I was being what ma would have called facetious.

"We have room, but I suggest you gentlemen retire to the rear of the hotel where you'll find a trough and soap. Dust off, wash up, then I'll be pleased to seat you, providing you have the wherewithal."

"That would be the cash, I presume?"

"That would be the cash," he said, looking down his nose as if he doubted it.

"We will return, when tidied up," I said and gave him my back.

We did return, and were seated with a large mug of foamy beer in front of us—I was still trying to acquire a taste for the stuff—when a young man, not too many years older than me and as well dressed as the fellow who greeted us, walked over.

"Welcome to Bidwell's, gentlemen," he said and stuck out his hand. I shook with him and then he took his chances putting a hand in Tiny's big paw, then turned back to me. "I'm John Bidwell so if there's anything I can do, just give me a yell."

"Just don't burn the beefsteak," I said, and he gave me a nod. He couldn't have been much more than ten years my senior and owned all we could see. The sign as we rode into the little town said Rancho del Arroyo Chico, thirty thousand lush acres. Do not molest the native people, the Mechoopda. They were here long before us.

It seemed the young Mr. Bidwell was not one of those who wouldn't serve Celestials, Indians, Negroes or Mexicans. I wish I had more time to get to know him.

He walked away and took a seat with the other two patrons, who he seemed to know. I was pleased when a young man in a white apron delivered us the bill of fare, as a beefsteak was only two dollars; oysters, which I'd heard of but never partaken, were two bits a piece.

I tried one and discovered it to be only two bites—and not to my taste. So, two bits wasn't a bargain at that.

Bidwell walked back over about the time I had a grimace from chewing the gray seafood.

"First time to down an oyster?" he asked and smiled.

"Yes, sir. Not to my taste, however."

"That one's on me. They are an acquired taste. You fellas heading up to the Bidwell's Bar?"

"No, sir, heading for San Francisco with a load of goods."

"Keep a sharp eye out. We've had more than one report of road agents. One Californio fella…"

"Californio?" I asked.

"Here before the revolution. One of the old families, Comacho is the family name. Has lost their holding down near Stockton in a card game and he's trying to recover the family fortune by taking it from those of us who came late. And his bunch don't say hands up. They just shoot and then see what the pickin's are. So be careful."

"Thanks for the warning," I said and meant it. "And thanks for allowing us in your fine establishment."

"Our pleasure. We value the law abiding and so long as that's you, you're always welcome."

I admired young Mr. Bidwell. Seemed an honest sort, one who'd won his fortune by hard work and didn't lord it over those less fortunate. We left, full and happy—Tiny's steak covered his plate—and I bid Mr. John Bidwell well, to risk what my Ma would call a pun.

It was only twenty-three miles, or so said the folks at Rancho del Arroyo Chico, to Ophir City, but we had the Feather River to cross. I was set on making it in one day, so I toed Tiny away before daylight, and we had a few slices of bacon and some hardtack and packed up before the sun was anywhere near topping the Sierras.

The country to the east, the Sierra foothills, was chopped up with black lava flows that I was glad we were not traversing. I knew that kind of country from much we crossed not far from where the Snake River poked out of the Teton country on our crossing on the Oregon Trail. Those lava rocks were sharp as razors and would cut up your animal's hocks and cripple them in short order were you not careful as a cat foraging in a wolf den.

But we made good time and were on the banks of the Feather River, looking at Ophir City just as a few oil lamps were being lit.

There was a ferry, but the ferryman wanted a dollar apiece to haul us over, and that galled me something awful. So, I told him I'd just wait until the light of day and swim my animals across.

We built us a fire a hundred feet off the trail near the river, and dang if he didn't hot foot it over just before the last light faded with yellow streaks in the sky to the west.

"If y'all still want to cross, I'll haul you over for two dollars. I gotta cross back anyhows."

"If you gotta cross anyway, how about a dollar?" I asked.

"Fine. I'm tired. You two pull."

He looked a little hangdog, but I couldn't help but give him a big smile.

Tiny pulled us over—five mules, two horses, packs, a heavy load, and the three of us—like we were an oak leaf blowing on the water. When we lit on the far side, the ferryman stopped Tiny as he was leading his horse and train of two mules off.

"You want a job? You'd make a ferryman."

"On my way to see my mama," he said, then ignored the man as he continued to try and convince Tiny that he had a great future as a ferryman.

As we were only a hundred paces from the edge of town, and still a bit saddle sore, we led our animals on into town.

Then I was sorry we'd crossed. All hell broke loose as gunfire erupted from both sides of the mud street.

25

With the street filling with gun smoke and lead flying, I quickly changed directions and headed for an alley between the assayer's office and a stone building with a sign Miner's and Merchant's Bank. As soon as our string was out of the line of fire of the battle going on, I pulled the Sharps and hotfooted it back to the street, yelling at Tiny as I passed, "Watch the string, I'll watch our backs."

I waited at the corner tucked behind the cover of the bank's stone wall and peeked around. A half-dozen fellows who looked to be Mexicans were on the far side, and this side was lined with a dozen who appeared to be miners. A couple of townsmen in top hats were scattering for doorways.

Shots were still flying back and forth over the mud street. I saw a Mexican in a wide sombrero go down as his compadres ducked behind water troughs and posts holding up porches. I had no idea who was in the right or wrong, who were the good guys or bad, so I merely guarded my mule train and my employee. Not that he needed guarding as he had tied the mules and horse off to a rail at the rear of the bank and was headed my way with scattergun in hand.

I had already learned that Tiny wasn't one to run from a fight, and he was proving it again.

He sidled up to me and, after taking a look at the street and the battle, asked, "Whose side are we on?"

"Ours," I said, and pulled him back out of the line of fire. "Let 'em fight it out."

And we did, and it didn't take long. Two of the Mexicans were on the ground, one trying to drag himself away down the boardwalk, the other on hands and knees in the mud street, his head hanging. One of the miners was on his back on the boardwalk, unmoving. The other Mexicans had scattered, one into a saloon, the other down an opening between buildings. The other two apparently had hightailed it as soon as the shooting started.

Another man in city clothes and a fashionable low-brimmed top hat was running down the street, splattering mud as he came. As he neared, I saw he had a star on his waistcoat, which was unbuttoned in the heat.

"I'm City Marshal Quinton. What the hell is going on?" he yelled from the middle of the street. The miners stepped out and walked to him.

I turned to Tiny. "Go back and guard the cargo," and I followed into the street wondering myself what had started this ruckus.

Four of the miners ran across the street, disarmed the two wounded Mexicans and pushed one flat on the boardwalk and the other one face down in the mud street.

A burly miner seemed to be the spokesman. "By all that's holy, Sheriff, we were in the Crystal and them Mexes were at the bar, just jawing in that infernal lingo of theirs. Toby, over yonder, lying dead on the boardwalk, kinda shoved one aside after asking him to move, and they went loco yelling they'd had enough of gringos. Toby knocked one with a hard fist. His eyes spun like a wheel of chance, and the others dragged him out. We was peaceful then, sipping the Crystal's good whiskey, playing monte and another table playing faro. Then them greasers run'd back in through the batwings, two of them with pistols in one hand and by God French swords in the other. Stole 'em off dragoons, I'd guess. Another had a knife and a pistol, and the fourth with a single barrel scattergun. He let off just inside the doorway, and Jake the bartender took a load in the chest. He's on the floor inside in a pool of blood, and Norval Wittington is down with a knife wound and a slash on the arm."

The marshal sighed deeply. "Norval gonna live?" he asked.

"I'd guess."

"Somebody go for the sawbones. When Doc Armstrong finishes with our kind, send him to the jail. If those two wounded greasers are still alive, he can tend them. Judge Wilkens is down in Sacramento due back in a few days, then we can try and hang 'em."

Then he instructed some of the miners to drag or carry the two wounded men to the jail.

The burly miner stopped the marshal as he started to follow. "Four of 'em ran off. One of them what run was the one who shot Jake down. And Jake with a wife and four young'uns. Shouldn't we go fetch 'em back to face the rope?"

"Let's get these two locked up and I'll get the sheriff after them. The county is his, and you can be dang sure they're on the run, way out of my jurisdiction."

I still had fifty dollars in gold so I found the livery and made a deal to stable the stock out behind his barn and grain them for fifty cents each if Tiny and I could sleep in his hay, to which he agreed. I found the banker, on the street where men were gathered, jawing about the gun-fight and made a deal with him to stow our packs inside the bank for a dollar. It was a sturdy stone building with an iron door and shutters. Tiny and I found ourselves in the Crystal saloon, celebrating the fact we weren't one of those shot down or those waiting for a trial. The Crystal offered thick slices of bread, sliced ham, mustard, oyster sauce, bowls of beans, and all the goober peanuts you could munch, so long as you were buying drinks. Oysters were available for four bits apiece, but I passed and would have were they free. Tiny and I both had a beer, which to my surprise, I was gaining a taste for. At two bits a glass, it was a cheap way to eat. Tiny must have eaten a loaf of bread and a pound of ham, so it was more than merely cheap.

But as most the men were downing whiskey at four bits for two fingers high, I could see how the saloon could afford the grub.

We found our way back to the livery after finishing our grub and suds, and I don't think I had much more than closed my eyes before I was dreaming of tall stands of wheat and corn on my place back in Oregon.

My dreams were interrupted by the shouts of men out in the street, so I pulled on my boots and charged out to see why the shouts and torches. I joined in a procession and asked the nearest miner, "What's going on?"

"They brought in two of those other four murderin' Mexicans, and we ain't waitin' for Judge Wilkins when we're the jury anyhows, so we done passed our verdict."

I followed along, staying off to the side, as most the men in the crowd of more than fifty covered their faces with bandanas. At the end of the street was a board and batt building attached to a sturdy stone one. The stone one had windows with bars—obviously a jail.

The city marshal was out on the boardwalk in front of a door with a sign painted on a glass portion of the door, that announced City Marshal. But he had been disarmed and his hands tied behind. His head was covered with a flour sack. He was yelling but hard to understand in the roar of angry men.

As I stood back in the shadows, miners and townsmen dragged four frightened Mexicans out and down the street to the edge of town. The wounded two could barely walk, but the ones brought in struggled to no avail.

I don't abide by folks taking the law, such as it is in the gold rush towns, into their own hands. But I was not about to voice my complaints to over fifty armed and angry men, many of those friends of the two dead fellows.

They had two reatas with hangman's knots, taking the thirteen turns, in each end of the leather woven ropes and slung the centers over a low limb of a live oak with a trunk three feet across.

I wondered what they waited for, then was a little surprised when they brought the two dead men—a thick-chested miner, and the bartender wearing a white shirt now mostly blood in the front with garters anchoring the sleeves—and leaned the dead men on the thick trunk. I guess they figured it was only just they witness the fate of those who'd shot them dead.

Then I was even more surprised to see them escort a woman and four stair-step children to the front of the crowd where they'd have a clear view.

The burly miner who'd done the talking to the marshal earlier, took a position in front of the four Mexicans, who were standing, trembling.

He yelled to the crowd. "No, by God you'll not shoot these bastards until we done hung 'em. Shoot them all you want after they stop kicking."

The crowd quieted, and he continued. "Okay, this is the official trial. Most of y'all saw what transpired down at the Crystal and out in the street. Raise your hands you think these greasers are guilty of assault, battery, murder, and being lower than snail slime or snakes' bellies."

More than half the men in the crowd raised their hands, as did the woman and four kids even though they'd not been anywhere near the Crystal.

The burly man turned to six men who'd taken positions behind the four Mexicans and said, "Put a strain on 'em." Three to a line, they started pulling on the center sections of the rope until all four Mexicans were kicking and strangling.

Even though I was sure they were guilty of heinous acts, my stomach roiled, and I tasted bile. I choked and spat into the street and looked away until the yells and shouts quieted, and men began walking away.

I took one glance back over my shoulder to see four miserable looking men, two with tongues hanging loosely; all four with heads canted to the side.

While others headed for their choice of the town's seven saloons, I went straight back to my hay pile.

Tiny was awake and sat up in his bedroll, and I crawled into mine.

"You don't look so good," Tiny said.

"They hung the four of them. No trial, just a lot of drunk men claiming to be a jury. Fact is, I believe it would make anyone ill."

We were lined up and waiting at the bank when it opened. Packs safe and sound, I paid the dollar I promised and by fifteen minutes after eight o'clock, we were clomping out of town—probably the fastest we'd ever loaded the string.

Yuba City is the next touch of civilization, a small berg

on the confluence of the Yuba and Feather Rivers. All that water flows to the Sacramento, and the Sacramento to San Francisco. I'm told it ain't much as towns go, but it is the farthest north the real steamboats travel. There's a chance we can catch a ride all the way to San Francisco and find ourselves where all we have to worry about are a load of failed miners and some tough river men.

If you can call that all?

26

It's just a little over thirty miles to Yuba City and flat dang near all the way. But too far to drag mules one stretch unless we want to travel at night. Seeing how many folks seem to operate outside the law in California, I don't think it wise. We cut off our day's ride at only fifteen miles as we came on the Feather River and had to cross. The ferryman wanted a dollar a critter, including the two of us, to pole us across, but I watched him haul a freight wagon and his pole never sank more than four feet. I eyeballed up and down the river and saw it widened by half again not far upstream. Logic said it was even more shallow there. So, I passed, and we worked our way two hundred yards upstream.

With the exception of one deeper channel no more than ten feet wide where the mules and our horses had to swim, we crossed easily nearly fifty yards in width.

We found a ready-made fire ring in a meadow on the far side, and it nearly a hundred fifty paces off the main trail. It suited me fine. The river had delivered plenty of driftwood to a nearby sand spit, so we soon had a cook-fire down to coals. As hot as it was, there sure wasn't a need for heat, although we were happy to dry our packs and bedrolls near a hot fire before we went to cooking. While things dried, and as we were early, we caught a few grasshoppers and soon had four fat trout popping in bacon grease. It was a feast after dining in smoky saloons or on side pork for so long—if you ignored Bidwell's plate-size steaks.

The next day we clomped into Yuba City, and observed a small single-story hotel, a mercantile, a tonsorial parlor—I'd get a shave and haircut but the man wanted a full dollar—a livery, and a dozen or so houses and cabins scattered beyond.

But the building that caught my interest had a large sign painted in red on a yellow background, which said, Steamship. As I neared, I could read a smaller sign, Flatboats for passengers and goods to Leodocia via Feather to Sacramento Rivers and points south. Steamboat, passenger cabins and steerage, freight and stock, to Sacramento City, California's Capital - Benicia, Vallejo, Oakland (Encinal), and San Francisco, connections to far flung. Steamboat boards at 11:00 a.m. daily.

We camped near the confluence of the Yuba and the Feather Rivers, not fifty feet from a dozen Argonauts who were obviously on their way to the diggin's, as they were still full of piss and vinegar and sang well into the night. They even erected a sign, The Nearly Rich Company. They invited us to join them, but I declined. We had purchased a loaf of fresh bread, paid four bits apiece for four eggs and fried them up with the last of our bacon for supper. As there were several groups of miners camped up and down the Yuba, I made my fake bedroll near the fire, but slept forty feet away with only my coat as cover. Tiny slept among the packs. It was a precaution I'd taken as a habit. A prowler would presume the lump of bedroll was me, and should one sneak the camp, he'd be surprised to find me in the darkness with my scattergun or Sharps in hand.

Luckily, morning arrived without any night visitors.

I immediately saddled Sandy, left Tiny drinking coffee and guarding our goods and headed for the Steamship company.

I found them open even though not yet 7:00 a.m. A half-dozen stevedores already were at work on the dock, sorting goods and readying a flatboat for departure.

The proprietor did not surprise me when he informed me it would be fifty dollars each for Tiny and me, and another twenty-five each should we want to transport our two horses. I described our five packs of goods and we agreed on another twenty-five dollars to the dock in San Francisco. I suggested to him I'd be happy to trade five mules and one horse for our passage and freight. He gave me a smile and informed me he'd have a herd of a hundred mules and horses were he allowed to make that deal. So, I gave him a ten-dollar Liberty to reserve our place on the eleven o'clock steamship, which was yet to arrive, and headed back to camp.

We packed up and headed for the livery. I negotiated, for at least an hour, with a gentleman name of Snodgrass, with a mane of gray hair. A sharp-featured fellow, he reminded me of pictures I've seen of President Andrew Jackson and was as foul-mouthed as Jackson was reputed to be. I walked away from our negotiating four times but returned as I needed to sell the mules and the Sorrel. [Disconnect: He made a deal with Mr. Bones for the sorrel earlier (page 131) so it should not be there any longer.] I wasn't about to give up Sandy as he had earned his place as a member of my family. We finally settled on forty dollars each for the mules, including their pack saddles, and twenty for the plow horse and his tack. So, he followed us to the steamship office where we unloaded the panniers from the mules.

I had to smile when the Lawrence came chugging up against the current. She was nothing like the mighty steamboats I'd seen on the Missouri and Mississippi, or even those that worked out of Lewiston on the Snake. She was sixty-five feet with a twelve-foot beam, a single stack for her steam engine, and a single sidewheel. The sign had said cabins, when, in fact, there was a single cabin for passengers, and it had only two single bunks. Maybe other ships had more.

Sandy was ground-tied to a deck ring in the aft, his stall made from stacks of crates, most empty as the freight had been delivered. He did enjoy the treat of a nosebag and was given an apple by Captain E. C. M. Chadwick, who was a serious man, I soon discovered, as he was constantly on the lookout for snags in the river. In these narrow channels if a boat sank it would put every business upstream at a hardship, and likely get the captain and crew of an ill-fated sunk obstacle in the river lynched.

Chadwick had a crew of four, one of which was always stationed on the bow, searching the water for snags and sandbars.

With the exception of Captain Chadwick, who sported a perfectly trimmed Van Dyke beard, they were a rough-looking raggedy bunch. The first mate reminded me of a skinny grizzly with enough hair on his shoulders and arms to occlude any view of skin. He wore a sleeveless pullover, overalls, and brogans with holes in the toes that appeared to have been inflicted with the Arkansas toothpick he wore in a scabbard on a leather belt. He was distinguished by the fact he had one ear sawed off down to the hole. The other three were equally roughshod and sour-breathed. Even though I objected, but not soon enough, two of the roustabouts, as they were called, loaded our packs. I could see they were surprised by the weight and gave me a curious look that I contrived to be evil.

I announced, "Bullet lead," when I got the look, and got a nod in return, but I could sense they were not convinced.

Chadwick informed me he'd had sixty Argonauts aboard on the trip up and not room for another skinny miner. Only two other passengers accompanied us on the sojourn downstream. They were speaking a language I surmised was French, and discovered when chatting with them they were, in fact, Belgian. One, a silver haired gentleman, informed me he was a mining engineer who'd been hired to judge the worth of a discovery, his companion was his assistant.

We laid over tied to the dock at Sacramento City, next to a sailing brig that had its masts and gear removed, was permanently attached to the dock with hinged planking to abide the rise and fall of the river, and I learned from the Captain, had been converted to a prison ship. Flat iron-barred square ports had been cut into the hull. I soon learned that many of the several hundred ships in San Francisco harbor had been converted to shore-like facilities, some of them even towed ashore now with street addresses, and now you'd have to go into the structures to determine they may have formerly visited Callao, Peru, or Shanghai, China.

As we docked, Tiny informed me he needed to go ashore to find an apothecary as he was having stomach pains. I handed him a ten-dollar Liberty. He thanked me and pocketed it. As they put out the gangplank, he hurried away. At the same time, we had what Captain Chadwick announced was a freak summer storm, and it began to rain.

Had I slept outside on a clear night I supposed the crew would not have found it strange. In the rain, they gave me strange looks as I spread my bedroll beside Sandy's makeshift paddock and atop my packs.

As it got dark, I became concerned that Tiny had not returned. Concerned for him and concerned that I could not alternate staying awake and guarding our trust.

Damn if the riverboat travel wasn't as concerning as a trail peppered with road agents.

27

I had a fitful night, finally leaving my bedroll stuffed with gear from my packs so it would appear I'd merely pulled the cover over my head. I moved off to a spot where I could nuzzle between the packs using my unneeded coat for a pillow and sleep with some confidence. Flies pestered me some, but the mosquitos must have been on vacation.

Awaking just before dawn, I sensed someone near, and when my vision cleared, I made out one of the roustabouts digging into one of our packs. I studied him for a moment, and realized it was the lout with the missing flapper over his ear hole. As he dug around, he glanced at my bedroll every few seconds. As I had one of my two scatterguns at my side, I rose silently and jammed the barrels into his side hard enough to break a rib.

He yelled and stumbled away.

"You lose something?" I demanded.

He eyed me, then the bedroll, then me again, rubbing his side as he did. Like the others he had a generous sized knife in his belt, but was wise enough not to put a hand on the hilt.

"I…I…I thought that was my…my pack," he mumbled.

"I assure you it's not. And the next time one of you louts runs a hand into one of my packs, I'm gonna blow it off. Understand?"

He took umbrage at that and puffed up like a toad. "I said it was an honest mistake."

"And I said what would happen next time. In fact, you get five feet from my goods your guts will be feeding the fish."

"You're mighty tough for a whelp holding a scattergun on a fella."

"Two scatterguns, a Colt, two hunting knifes, and a Sharps so I'm likely as tough as all you louts." I didn't mention the two belly guns. One never knows…

"So you say…"

"I do, and I wonder if you can convince the captain you thought that was your pack."

He glared at me but spun on his heel.

He wasn't on deck come light, and Captain Chadwick came asking about him.

After I described my run-in with earless, he nodded and added, "A worthless sogger, so no loss." Then he questioned, "Your friend, that big fella, not back yet?"

"I haven't seen him, so no."

"We'll be casting off in thirty minutes, no matter."

"I understand." As I replied, I saw Tiny at a brisk walk nearing the gangplank. I pointed, "No worry, Captain. You need help being shy a man?"

"We'll do fine. There's some sweet breads, smoked salmon caught right here on the river, and coffee below. Part of the service as we're short an eater and one of ours gave you some concern."

"Thank you. I'll partake soon as I parley with Tiny."

"Tiny? That's a laugh," he said, and I nodded in agreement.

The Captain excused himself as Tiny hurried aboard and to my side. "Sorry, Mister Zane."

"You find something for your stomach?" I asked, concerned.

"I did. Two things."

"Two?"

"Yes, some soda stuff at the apothecary and a Chinee girl to ride it for the rest of the night. She wouldn't let me be on top. Too big, she said. Only five dollars."

I couldn't help but laugh, then cautioned him, "The Captain would have left and left you had you not made it back."

He looked puzzled. "But I did make it back."

"Okay, no harm done. Let's go below. Captain said coffee and sweet breads and smoked fish. By the way, you owe me ten dollars."

He smiled. "Take it out of my wages. I had me some breakfast, but I could eat again."

"Why am I not surprised?" I said and led him to the ladder.

As we chugged down the Sacramento, going almost due south, Captain Chadwick informed me that we'd soon bear southwest, then due west, not that we had a choice as our road was the river. My feet were propped up on an empty keg, my butt on my rolled-up coat on another, and not a lick of dust was blowing in my face. It wasn't cool, in fact, still sweatin' hot, but there was a breeze, and the breeze made it hard for the skeeters to light. So far, this makes the trail look like a rocky cliff as opposed to smooth sand spit. This could spoil a fella.

We'll make one stop—Smith's Landing. The town, he tells me, was almost totally wiped out with a plague not long after it was founded, but it's safe now. It's a waypoint for passing Argonauts on their way to the diggin's.

The river is moving at a brisk six knots, sometimes slowing where it widens, but not much, and we make six knots with our sidewheel and little steam engine. We're fairly flying. I'm impressed as we pass a boat, a sidewheeler, at least three times our size, the Wilson G. Hunt. Chadwick informs me she'll do fifteen knots, and I thought we were flying. Of course, upstream she's only making an overland speed of nine knots.

I'm told we're a tad over one hundred miles on the water, down the Sacramento, into San Pablo Bay that's actually the north half of the same body of water that is San Francisco Bay.

Now that old one ear had jumped ship, the others seemed to pay no mind to my packs, but nonetheless, as we had an overnight at Smith's Landing, Tiny and I would trade off with two-hour watches. He'd proven to be a fine companion, even though he wasn't much company, didn't talk much, and I suspected, his bad stomach was an excuse to find a soiled dove.

The Sacramento has many islands and side channels, and it's obvious the Captain has to be a real river pilot in order to keep us afloat and not stranded on a bar or stabbed and sunk with a snag. By the number of logs on the shore, it's clear high water brings some massive ones down out of the high country.

As the Lawrence slows and approaches the dock at Smith's Landing, I give a whistle to Tiny and wave him over from his spot flat on his back on the deck, feet up on a railing.

He looks a bit irritated that I've disturbed his repose, but he lumbers to his feet and comes my way.

"Tiny, we're coming into town, such as it is. If your stomach starts growling for another slice of soiled dove, you're gonna have to satisfy yourself with some smoked salmon or maybe ask Captain Chadwick to share a chunk of a big old sturgeon they caught."

"Who would eat a big ol' surgeon?"

I have to laugh. "Not a doctor, Tiny, a big river fish. A sturgeon. You gotta go down to the galley and see this beast. He's five feet long."

"No?" Tiny said, doubting me.

"Yes. And it's said they grow to three times that and can weigh as much as a horse." He's looking at me like I should become a guest in an asylum, so I laugh and slap my thighs. "Ask Captain Chadwick, you doubt me."

"You're funnin' me," he said, looking at me with his head cocked.

"No, sir, I'm not, so don't be falling in the river. As even as big as you are, one of them big sturgeon fish could likely swallow you whole."

"Bull," he said, head still cocked.

"You're staying aboard tonight. Maybe I can borrow a Bible from Captain Chadwick and you can read about Jonah getting swallowed by a big ol' fish."

"Can't read."

"Then I'll read it to you."

"Not going ashore?"

"I know, your stomach is starting to bother you. Forget it, I'm the boss man and I'm not loaning you another Liberty. So, you might as well stay aboard."

He shrugged and returned to his spot. Then one of the roustabouts yelled at him to lend a hand, and he helped winch the gangplank to the dock. The dock was jam packed with Argonauts, but all but three were headed upstream, and those three came aboard. They were dressed in brocaded waistcoats with brass buttons but unfastened, as warm as it was, particularly now that we'd stopped moving over the water. They each had on those low half-height top hats with what I'd always thought were worthless narrow brims, canvas trousers tucked into boots, and red sashes around their waists tied near the side with over a foot of tail hanging. The hats were fancy, but a little beaten and bent.

They ignored Tiny and me, after giving us a look like we were something to be shoveled out of a stall and headed to the very bow and stacked some empty crates, throwing some aside. Two of which landed atop my pile of packs.

They really hadn't hurt anything, but it was a bit on the rude side as there was plenty of open deck nearby.

I decided to shrug it off, but Tiny seemed to take umbrage, walked forward and threw the crates off our goods.

The biggest of the three, with a pockmarked face and a nose that was not only crooked but smashed flat, looked over his shoulder and glared at Tiny then to my surprise. As even as big as he was, Tiny was equally tall and outweighed him by fifty pounds.

"We botherin' you, Gordo?" the man said.

Tiny stood with hands on hips. "My name's not Gordo, folks call me Tiny."

"Tiny. Tiny brain maybe." He and his friends all guffawed. Then flat-nose continued, "Gordo means fat, Mister No Brain, and boy are you fat, mate."

"My name's not Mister No Brain or Not Mate," Tiny said, his brow furrowed.

"Fine, not mate," flat-nose said. I couldn't quite figure his accent, a little English, a little Irish maybe, then he explained it. "You ever hear of the Sydney Ducks, Not Mate?"

Australians. I'd heard talk of the Australians who called themselves Sydney Ducks, and none of what I'd heard was any dang good. They were the curse of young San Francisco, if talk could be believed.

Tiny seemed confused with the "not mate" crack and was shaking his head.

"I heard of lots of kinds of ducks, but not no Sydney ducks."

"Well, Not Mate, I'm a Sydney Duck, and we're the toughest most killin' gang in all California, so, when I throw somethin' somewhere, you leave it there." While flat-nose talked, he slipped a hand in a pants pocket and it came out with some device I believe my pa had told me about, brass knuckles, as I recall he'd called them. He held the hand at his side, slightly behind his thigh so Tiny couldn't see the flash of the brass, but I could.

Tiny was starting to get the fact he was being talked down to, and I could see him beginning to redden. The group was well armed, each with a revolver on one hip and a sixteen-inch knife on the other. The other two, watching amusedly, stood back, smiling. Neither of them had front teeth, which told me that fighting was likely a habit among them.

Tiny looked over at me, I think taking some confidence in the fact he knew I stood with scattergun in hand, but with muzzles still pointed at the deck.

Tiny yelled at me, serious as could be, "Mister Zane, you think he means to do me hurt?"

28

My gaze drifted from the big man confronting Tiny to the other two and back, before I answered, "Tiny, he looks like a smart fella, even if he doesn't know he's a Homo sapien not a dang duck, so I can't imagine he's dumb enough to give you trouble. But if he does, you pick him up and sling him overboard and maybe one of those big sturgeon fish will take a chomp outta his gordo butt."

"What in the bloody hell is a Homo sapien?" flat-nose mumbled. Now it was the duck's turn to look confused. For the first time, the big boy realized we were together. He gave me a dismissive look, but I'd been standing, like him, holding my weapon out of sight. I figured this was a good time to let him know the odds were a little more even than he realized, and I brought the double barrel into sight and raised the barrels about halfway to level.

His dismissive look turned to a wide grin. "You fellas headed for San Fran, like us, I guess. We should get to know each other."

I shook my head slowly. "That might normally be just fine, mate, but we got business to take care of, and it doesn't involve quacking with some ducks, even if them ducks are the toughest and most killin' in San Francisco. So, let me spare you getting your noggin knocked off by my associate, Tiny, and advise you to take your mates and head back to the stern."

"Gets all the smoke and embers and such back there. I believe…"

"You believe," I snapped, and raised the muzzles a few inches higher, "that you'll find yourselves a nice spot on the stern." I cocked both barrels, then added, "Those brass gizmos you snaked outta your pocket would'a just made Tiny angry, and he'd likely jerk both your wings off and flung them to the fishes as well as your noggin."

He returned the brass knuckles to his pocket, and waved to his two associates, who followed him around the deckhouse. He turned back right before he was out of sight. "Them packs is your business?" he asked.

"My business is my business," I replied. He nodded and they disappeared to the stern.

Thinking on it, I think I let my sturgeon-mouth overload my minnow-backside. I should never have made those three think I had some special business at hand. I should have let them think I was busted and heading home to Boston town with my tail between my legs.

I'm hoping that mouthing too much prideful arrogance doesn't cost me dearly.

Pa told me more than once, pride goes before a fall.

***

There were two cafes in Smith's Landing, both only strides from the dock, one of which sported a sign that said Chi's Celestial Café, and the other Lopez Familia Food and Cervesa, but we couldn't both leave our goods, particularly with three now angry Ducks aboard. So, I flipped a coin with Tiny, after making him promise that if he won and got to disembark to eat and bring me back some supper, he wouldn't wander away and try to talk a brothel into selling him a lady's time and attention for the last two dollars he had to his name.

He called the toss, and I won, so I didn't have to worry. The deal was whoever went could choose from Chi's or the Lopez family. I chose Lopez. It would be dark before I returned, but Captain Chadwick was still in his wheel-house, so I wasn't too worried. I'd mentioned to him our little run-in with the Ducks and he had suggested to them they remain aft as he wanted no trouble on board.

The fare was rice, beans, something called tamales, which was chicken in some dough, and to my great surprise, a lamb's head that had been slow roasted and covered with some dark brown sauce. It was excellent, but so dang pepper-hot it toasted my taste buds before I got it a fourth eaten. I managed to down two of the half-dozen tortillas the size of the top of a beer keg, as they and the beer seemed to quiet the fire of the rest of the meal. And speaking of beer, I learned there was a fine cooper somewhere near as I bought a small oak keg with wooden bung, holding no more than a gallon, with the promise I'd return it before we sailed. I learned that Cervesa, as the sign announced, was beer, in the Spanish language the Lopez family spoke. I kept my consumption to a single mugful, with the thought I'd treat Captain Chadwick and his crew to a mug, even though we hadn't been invited to partake of roast sturgeon. Our trip didn't include meals, so I had nothing to complain about except for the high price of three dollars for the meal and another dollar for the beer.

I barely dented the lamb's head so spent an extra quarter for a muslin towel to wrap it, purchased an extra serving of rice and beans, and was loaned two peach tins to transport them, and a wooden spoon. I had a pile of four tortillas left which would serve as a wrapper so really didn't need the spoon, but had promised to return tins, spoon, and keg and headed back the hundred paces to the Lawrence with my arms full.

Tiny was perched on a rail, scattergun in hand, looking a little forlorn, but smiled when he saw the abundance of supper. He smiled even more broadly when I poured one of the tin cups we had from our packs full of beer. Then he frowned when I headed for the ladder to take the rest of the keg to Chadwick and the crew.

I was not particularly pleased when one of the boat's roustabouts was on the stern with the Sydney Ducks, and I was suspect about what they were talking about, as all four eyed me when I topped the ladder and headed to the bow.

Tiny and I alternated standing guard through the night, with my caution to him to be extra vigilant.

But the sun rose, and the steam engine slowly creeped to life with no reason to use our scatterguns.

I barely had time to return the tins, spoon, and empty keg before we cast off. It was quite a sight when, in early afternoon, we passed Benicia, the capital of California, on the north bank, which seemed a thriving if small town, then through narrows that the Captain announced was Carquinez Straits with rocky oak covered shoulders to the south and rolling grassy hills to the north. This opened into a wide bay that, even in early afternoon, had a layer of fog. I only knew it to be a bay as the Captain kept up an interesting narrative as we proceeded.

San Pablo Bay, the north half of the body of water commonly called San Francisco Bay.

For the first time, as we neared the bay, we experienced chop, waves of only a couple of feet, but with the wind in our face, capped with white. We enjoyed the drop in temperature and what was now salt-spray cooling our faces.

For the first time in my seventeen years, soon to be eighteen, I tasted the salty sea.

Chadwick yelled down from the wheelhouse. "Zane, you and Tiny stand the bow. Larboard and starboard and keep a sharp eye. This damnable fog can be the death of us."

"Rocks, islands, what?" I yelled back.

"Hell no, ships and boats and barges and anchor lines. Changes every time I cross. Get to it."

"Yes, sir," I yelled back, and Tiny and I hurried to our post. It would be a hell of a note to get this close to San Francisco, only to drown in a shipwreck.

29

We chugged across the bay, then found ourselves picking our way between ships of all size and variety—ghost ships. Long three-masted, full-rigged sailing ships of two hundred or more feet, brigs, brigantines, barks, schooners, side-and stern-wheelers, and smaller ketches and sloops.

It was both a beautiful and sad sight and would soon be a dangerous one, as they were mostly crewless and without lamps in the fading light. I admired our Captain's deft movements through ships and anchor lines. All were anchored with sails furled. As beautiful as many were, it was a chilling sight. All that power and enterprise, dead in the water.

Just as light was about to fail and an Island was on our starboard—Angel Island the Captain said, then another, Alcatraz Island—we poked our nose out of the fog, and out of the colony of dead ships. I felt as if we were exiting a graveyard and each vessel a headstone or crypt—but a city came alive before us. Ships had been winched ashore to serve as saloons and shops, brick and masonry build-ings were built and windows lit and others on the rise, and beyond, for as far as I could see in the fading light, the hillsides were blistered with tents. Many of them lighted now with coal-oil lanterns, a few lit and silhouetted from camp and warming fires—it was cool for the first time since leaving the pass between the Klamath and the Sierra Range.

As I looked up the street rising ahead of us, I could see masts and booms had been converted to cranes and were now lifting building materials as high as five stories to men who were swinging hammers or hauling mortar to masons whose trowels flashed lantern light.

As we neared the dock, the air rang with men shouting, beer and freight wagons clattering, buggies serving as cabs and personal transportation ringing iron tires on cobblestones, and horse backers clomping. Everywhere along the quay, even at near dark, men were at work loading what were mostly river vessels or ferries to cross the bay.

The roustabouts threw lines to their equals ashore and while they tied us off, securing us to a dock some six feet higher than our deck, I could hear music—a blather as there was more than one source—coming from saloons and bawdy houses.

Chadwick strode up next to me. "It's a sight, is it not? You're looking at the Barbary Coast, lad. Hardly more than three years ago she was a Mexican village called Yerba Buena, and the whole of what is now California had maybe thirty thousand. Since then over two hundred thousand from the world over have tromped through here."

"How big is the city now?" I asked.

"More population than the whole of California had before the siren call of gold. And there's more a' coming."

As I stared out at the city, I couldn't help but ask, "So,

you think a young chap like myself should invest his wages in pick and pan and head back to the diggin's?"

He gave me a long look and took time for a deep sigh. "You saw all them dead ships we passed. Every mother's son jumped ship and left their employers and captains and headed to muck in the mud. The fact is, son, only those blessed by pure luck will go home with more than a pot to piss in. The real money is mining the miners and always has been in a rush like this. Take the sure money; and that's trading those fellas doing the mucking out of theirs. You see me on the wheel, not on a rocker."

"I do, and I thank you for the advice. How long can I leave my packs onboard?"

"I'm out of here with the incoming tide, to push me back to the Sacramento, and that begins at six twenty-seven in the morning. We'll cast off about seven fifteen. You should make sure your goods are off by seven."

"I appreciate that. Can you give me directions to the Niantic Hotel?"

He laughed. "You're gonna be eating high on the hog, youngster, you dine at the Niantic."

"No, sir, got some business with a fella there. I'll be leaving Tiny aboard to watch our goods, if that's fine with you?"

"Fine as frog's hair, son. You wantin' a Humpback steak?"

"Sir?"

"The Niantic was a whaler a'fore she was towed ashore to have three stories built atop her decks. She burned to the ground and has been rebuilt so you won't have to put up with the smell of rendering down fat."

I had to chuckle at that, then asked, "How do I find her?"

"Four blocks up that away. You can't miss her. But, beware, twixt here and there, and in every crack and cranny in San Fran, is a swindler, a grafter, and someone who'll try and steal your long Johns or the brogans off'n your treaders. Keep a sharp eye."

I thanked him, and he headed for his wheelhouse and passed the three Sydney Ducks who were headed my way. My scattergun was forward with Tiny, but I lay a hand on the butt of my Colts.

"Well, if it ain't the lippy shoat," the flat-nose one said, but stopped six feet from me as I was already hoisting the revolver. I remained with it half out of the holster as he continued to mouth off. "You'll be in my alleys and shadows now, lippy. And wherever you're headed with all them goods, you ain't gonna make. I'll throw a spanner in your works no matter which way you turn. You'll be arse-over-tit in no time."

"Then maybe," I said, lifting the Colt another inch or so, "I ought to hole a couple of your hides while you're not skulking in the shadows."

He laughed, but headed for the gangplank, and I spun on my heel and moved Tiny's way. I was pleased to see him not ten feet distant, his big bulk between some crates, a scattergun in hand. He let the hammers down as I confronted him. "Got to go and find this Lord Willard Stanley-Smyth, get him to pick up his goods and pay us off. You got the duty until I return."

I felt a little like I was going into the jaws of the dragon as I gazed up the street into the bustling city. I'd long heard about what a den of dangerous lowlifes resided there, working honest folks innocently passing through to try and make their fortune, out of their hard-earned. I had not seen a city a fourth the size, or a hundredth as busy as San Francisco, so I vowed to be extra careful and wished I had a couple more fellas to guard our goods. But I didn't and had to find Lord Willard Stanley-Smyth. The Sharps was the most formidable weapon I had, other than the scatterguns, but to fire a scattergun in that mess of flesh in the streets would likely take who you shot at along with two or three passersby. So, I gathered up the Sharps and pocketed some paper cartridges.

"I'm hungry," Tiny announced, which was about his most common explanation.

"Well, bless your little black heart. Ain't you always?"

"I don't have a black heart. That kinda hurts my feelings."

I can't help but laugh. "That's called kidding, Tiny. Fact is you're one of the kindest people I know and to prove it, and should I find this Lord, I'm gonna give you a twenty-dollar bonus on top your wages and forgive the ten dollars you owe me."

He looks at me curiously. "This Stanley-Smyth fellow. This Lord. He some kind of holy man?"

I was stumped for a second, then laughed. "No, Tiny. A Lord over in John Bull country is kinda like a senator in the States."

"Oh. Okay. You gonna bring me some vittles when you get back?"

"I will. You keep a sharp eye out. Captain Chadwick says there's a bandit behind every light pole."

"Wow, and there's lots of light poles."

I chuckled all the way off the Lawrence.

As I strode up the street, which had work going on even at this evening hour, mud replaced with cobblestones. Work, as seemed typical of all San Francisco. I noted that most of the buildings were restaurants and saloons. And all seemed boisterous with men, drinking, gambling, eating, and smoking. Music from a number of doorways blended to a cacophony of sound, pretty much nonsensical. It seemed outside of every public establishment, smoke roiled, and if you gazed inside, many looked to be fogged in down to the waist—smoke occluded.

I was approached by four different fellows, and one generous sized lady, on my trek up the low rise. And another bumped into me and I felt his hand slip inside my coat...I presume trying to pick my purse, but I had none. I shoved him hard and he bounced off the brick wall of a building with a sign announcing Pigs, Chickens, and Lamb, then ran before I could cuff him as I hoped to do. Two of those who slowed me wanted to direct me to accommodations, one to a den of opium pleasures, one to a house full of "lovely, fine-smelling, doves". Then there was the lady. Who was obviously a soiled dove herself, and soiled she was with red hair spiked with a comb and cheeks and lips reddened so much she looked clownish, particularly as she had smudges of dirt or coal dust on face and half-open blouse. Her melon-sized breasts were nearly exposed and ballooning up with some apparatus that created a canyon between into which a face would disappear should one be tempted to voyage there among the warts. Her offer was to lead me between buildings and let me give her a poke for a mere four bits. I politely passed, as I passed, even if enticed, I imagine it would be pox along with the poke.

As it happened, I was on the wrong side of the street from the hotel so needed to cross. One would think fifty feet an easy trek, but buggies, gigs, handsome cabs, horse backers, farm wagons loaded with produce and followed by loose hounds, beer wagons, and fellows afoot but tugging mules and donkeys, made it a bit of a challenge. Fellows shouting curses at their animals, chain traces clanging, iron tires singing and ringing on cobblestones, and wooden axles and harness leather groaning, made it hard to hear oneself think. As I dodged between a gig and a beer wagon, the wagon driver snapped a whip near my ear so close I thought I was shot, and I leapt two feet ahead.

I spun as he yelled, "Got no time to grease me wheels with you!"

So, I yelled back, raising the Sharps halfway up, "And I got no time to waste a ball on that fat gut."

He ignored me and clattered on past.

Now, to find Lord Willard and settle up.

30

There was a drawing of the original Niantic in the lobby of the rebuilt hotel, showing the prow sticking into the street, featuring a carved bare-breasted woman above the dolphin striker and below the prow. I believe they call that a figurehead. I wished I'd seen the hotel when she was a whale ship dragged ashore, before she'd burned.

But she was a sight as she was, as I was stopped by a doorman in a top hat with a walking stick topped by a brass lion head the size of my fist—as he shook it at me and pointed to a boot scraper I got the impression the stick was for more than just support.

"Kind sir," he said politely, although the scars over his eyes and his cauliflowered ear indicated he had not been so polite in past instances, "Please respect our carpets and clean your brogans."

I gave him a nod and returned the polite smile as I did so, then stepped inside double doors with oval glass inserts nearly their whole generous size. And saw his concern. Chinese carpets, featuring flowers and birds artfully woven, covered the floors between door and desk, off to the side were equally fancy doors separating the lobby from a saloon on one side and a restaurant on the other. A curved stairway, six feet wide, wrapped from the lobby over and behind the registration desk.

A slender fellow with a narrow mustache and greased hair, parted in the middle and flat above his high forehead, gave me a nod and a bit of a worried look as I sauntered over and lay both hands on the edge of the tall desk; teak I'd guessed.

"A room, sir?" he asked.

"No, sir, I'm to meet with a guest, Lord Willard Stanley-Smyth."

He eyed me carefully, with a smile tight as lizard lips, nodded before he spoke, "You and half the city of San Francisco would like to meet with Lord Stanley-Smyth. I'll be happy to send your calling card up to the Lord's suite. Suggest you..." he hesitated for a moment before he insulted me, "...wait outside. There's a bench out there."

"Calling card?" I said, having no idea what the devil he was talking about.

"Yes, young man. If you want to see Lord..."

"He wants to see me."

And, I noted, there were two benches inside. So, as I walked over, took a seat and picked up a Leslie's Weekly, I informed him, "I'll wait right here. I have a delivery for the Lord, and you can rest assured he'll come a'runnin', he knows I'm here."

"Humph," the officious clerk managed.

"Your name?"

"I'm Jake Zane, from Lewiston, here after a long trek to deliver goods to Lord Stanley-Smyth. You go fetch him and tell him I was hired by his man, Tennison."

"Tennison?"

"I don't have all night, so go fetch him or tell me where I can find him, and I'll go."

"Only guests are allowed up the stairs."

"I've come over a thousand miles, sir. To be truthful, I don't much give a damn if I'm allowed or not. Are you gonna fetch him or am I going to go from door to door until someone answers to the name?"

He rounded the desk, walked right by me and to the front doors. I thought he was going to call the old boy with his brass-headed shillelagh for assistance. I didn't want a dent in my noggin from that knob, so I rose and rested a hand on my Colt. Then was pleased when the desk clerk instructed the doorman to go up to the governor's suite and deliver my message to Lord Stanley-Smyth.

As he returned to his station, and the doorman headed for the stairs, the clerk instructed me, "Take a seat. His lordship is normally not in much of a rush."

I think he was surprised when a fellow I presumed, by his dress, to be the Lord, followed closely behind the doorman and strode across the Chinese carpets, as I stood, and extended his hand. He had on a four-in-hand tie over a starched white shirt, all under a cutaway black coat with fine white stripes. The trousers were fitted, and he wore white spats over polished black shoes. Pince-nez eyeglasses rested on the end of a patrician nose.

He introduced himself as did I, then he asked, "Where's Max?"

"Max?" I replied, then realized I'd only heard Tennison's first name, Maxwell, one time and that way back on the Snake.

"Sorry to deliver bad news, sir, but Mister Tennison took an Indian arrow through his neck, and we lost him in a very few minutes."

The Lord looked as if I'd slapped him hard with the flat of my hand. He rested a hand on my shoulder, then took a seat on the bench I'd been occupying and sunk his face into both hands.

Finally, he looked up, "And Gunter Stadt?"

"Stadt was shot dead with two holes in his back up on the trail, by road agents who we killed when coming into California. In a narrow, the pass between the Klamath and the Sierra ranges. Both of them, along with a couple of old mountain men fellas, one I knew only as Alabama, and the other Jasper Willoby. We buried them just off the trail as well. It was not a good trip."

"We buried?" he asked.

"We. I joined the crew in Lewiston after they lost and buried a shotgun guard there. There were six of us in the crew. Tennison, Stadt, Willoby, Alabama, Chang and myself. I left Chang, wounded and hopefully recovering, back in Leodocia. He was our cook and much more after we got thinned out to just Chang and me."

"And you brought my goods in?"

"I did, sir, with the help of a man I hired in Leodocia when Chang couldn't continue due to a shot-up shoulder."

"And where are my goods now?"

"Loaded onboard the sidewheeler, Lawrence, and they're still aboard at the wharf, just four blocks down the way, guarded by my man, Tiny. And I'd sure like to get them delivered and signed off to you."

He rose and snapped at the clerk. "Send someone to fetch a cab and a freight wagon. I'm taking Fellows with me."

The clerk shrugged and replied, "I'll have to send Fellows after the cab and wagon."

"Fellows?" I asked.

"The doorman. He's part-time a city marshal when needed for special events."

"Wait here," the Lord said. The clerk hurried out and sent the doorman running, as the Lord belied his obvious age and gray hair and took the stairs two at a time. The clerk returned to his station, and in a short time the Lord beat the doorman back to the lobby. Only this time, the Lord had a gun belt with a fancy engraved Colt on his hip.

"Let's go," he said. But Fellows wasn't back, so he turned to me and said, "Let's walk. He'll catch up." Then he stuck his head back in the door and yelled at the clerk. "Send my transportation and Fellows down to the Lawrence. We're going on..." And he hurried away, weaving through the crowded boardwalk, with me on his heels.

As we neared the wharf, where the Lawrence was tied up, I saw that another vessel, a sailing ketch was now tied alongside. From a half block up the hill, I thought nothing of it as the docksides were lined with ships and not a foot was available as far as I could see up and down the bay front.

And I couldn't see far as light was beginning to fade out in the bay, as the city was beginning to light with lamps behind us.

Then I realized the three Sydney Ducks and at least three more louts were busy passing our heavy packs from the Lawrence to aboard the ketch.

31

"Hold up, Lord," I snapped.

He stopped and turned.

"Trouble," I said. "We're being robbed."

He snapped back and eyed the ship. "That ketch?" he said.

"Yes, sir. They're passing the packs with your goods over."

"And your guard?"

"Don't see him."

"You any good with that Sharps. I believe it's the same one I gave my stepson."

"Tennison…Tennison willed it to me. I'll return…"

"No, you'll use it. I make it seventy-five yards to those blokes. I'm going on down there. You hold up over there," he pointed. "Use that light post to steady your aim. If anything happens to me, or if I give you a wave, use your weapon."

I nodded; glad I'd pocketed a half-dozen paper cartridges.

As he walked away, the Lord yelled back over his shoulder. "Stay alert, send Fellows with a warning when he shows up."

And he strode to the waterfront, out the dock, and down the gangway. The big Sydney Duck who'd threatened me, met him as he reached the gunnels.

I brought the Sharps to my shoulder. Because the Lawrence and the Ketch were below dock and quay level, I couldn't see all that was going on aboard either vessel but had a clear view of the flat-nose Sydney Duck now with his hand in the center of the Lord's chest. I couldn't hear a word of what was happening as I stood with the rifle steadied on the lamp post, when I got a tap on the shoulder. I didn't feel I could take my eyes off the boats, so merely snapped, "I'm busy here."

"I see that, and I'm a city copper. You shooting ducks or what?" he asked.

Had I not been a little busy I might have laughed with his statement, wrong but right only Sydney Ducks, not feathered ones. I glanced back. He was uniformed, with matching hat, blouse and trousers, but unarmed except for a cudgel as long as my forearm that he held in a hand even though his arms were crossed. His badge was round with a big centered 'SF' and smaller 'Police' below.

I looked him square in the eye so he'd have no doubt my seriousness. "Crime going on, Mister Copper. I'm the backup for Lord Stanley-Smith, who's on that gangway chatting with the fellas stealing his goods. Maybe you should leave me be and go lend him a hand."

"What?"

"Crime, if you're a lawman, get down there and enforce the law."

He didn't hesitate but moved at a trot.

Just as he reached the dock, I cursed myself as I shouldn't have been watching him but should have had my eyes on the decks.

A shot rang out, reverberating over the street noise, and the copper spun around and went down.

I scanned the boats and saw a man with a rifle atop the little deckhouse on the ketch. He didn't have time to wonder what happened to him, as the Sharps bucked in my hand and he flew backward, arms flailing, and off the deckhouse out of sight.

Reloading as quickly as I could, still watching the boats, I saw both the flat-nose Duck and the Lord draw at the same instant, but they were close enough that the Lord gave the Duck a hard shove and as the gunnel was more than a foot above the deck, when the Duck stepped back he lost his balance and fell.

Two of the other six Sydney Ducks I'd seen were jumping from ketch to Lawrence. Seeing them coming, both with pistols in hand, Lord Stanley-Smyth jumped off the gangplank into the bay and disappeared.

I got a cartridge seated and fired at the Duck in the lead and he was blown back against the deck house of the Lawrence, only to be gathered up by the big fella and shoved ahead and onto the ketch, followed by the third one.

Reloading as I watched, the third one got greedy and went for one of the remaining packs, weighing more than the eighty pounds of gold it carried, he seemed surprised as he tried to heft it.

He took a moment too long as I blew his brisket into splinters and he went to his back. This time I dropped a cartridge as I reloaded, realizing they were casting off the ketch from the Lawrence. Two of them were madly pushing her off with grappling hooks on long poles.

She obviously wasn't powered as she had no stack, and I was more concerned with Lord Stanley-Smyth than the escaping Sydney Ducks, for the moment. As I reloaded, I ran for the dock.

I knelt by the copper when I came even with him, but he'd taken one in the side just ahead of his left arm and I was sure it was a heart and lung shot. He was barely blowing bubbles through his lips, so I hustled to the edge of the dock and searched down between the Lawrence and the wharf.

"Over here," I heard a shout and turned to see him ascending a ladder leading up to the boardwalk that fronted the bay. "Don't let them get away," he yelled. I moved on down the dock until I came even with the ketch and the three remaining standing Sydney Ducks, two of whom were hoisting sail. The big one was on the wheel just ahead of the aft mizzenmast.

They were less than forty yards from me. I settled down in a prone position as the big Duck hoisted a revolver and started pulling off on me. His shooting platform was rocking, but mine was as steady as the earth. A shot splattered the dock not far from my head, blowing splinters into the right side of my face, causing me to misfire and my shot to go wild.

I rolled to my back and reloaded, trying of offer as small a target as possible. When I rolled back, I could see both mizzen and main sail were hoisted, and the ketch was turning into the wind. The Duck who'd hoisted the mizzen sail was standing aft, between me and the man on the wheel, much to his misfortune.

This time I was able to take my time, take a breath, and squeeze. The aft Duck, now a sailor if only for a very short time, flew forward into flat-nose who was on the wheel, knocking him aside. Without steerage, the wind took the ketch and spun it when the wheel was released, and it took a few moments to bring her back into the wind.

Too many moments, I'm sure the big Duck who'd

threatened me thought, as I was able to reload, and their escape hadn't taken them nearly far enough out of range.

"Kill the bugger," I heard over my shoulder and glanced back to see the Lord standing, dripping, with his arms crossed, looking very determined.

"No choice," I muttered, as I lay down on the big man who was now crouching down to offer as small a target as possible. But shoulders and head still showed. I was concentrating and didn't hear the footfalls on the dock. The Sharps bucked in my hands, and I heard someone yell, "No!"

And all went black.

32

I thought I was on the dock, by the bay. But as my eyes focused, I was staring at something going round and round. I closed them tightly again, which made my head hurt. Then I realized that every breath, every movement, every heartbeat, made my head hurt.

Then I realized I was surrounded by both men and women, and in bed.

I brought a hand up from under covers and shaded my eyes.

"Where am I?" I managed. Then realized the man bending over me was Lord Stanley-Smyth.

"Take it slow. You got a hell of a rap on the head from a copper. Sorry, I tried to stop him."

Then another face appeared. It was Tiny, and I breathed a sigh of relief. I was worried he was feeding petrel and crabs at the bottom of the bay. I saw a knot on his forehead, half the size of a hen egg.

"You okay, Tiny?" I asked.

"Them fellas snuck up on me. Sorry, young boss."

I managed to focus back on the Lord. "And the goods?"

"All accounted for," the Lord said with a smile. "You

blew a hole in the helmsman's head and the only one of those blokes left wasn't much of a sailor. The coppers had a steam-driven harbor boat nearby and caught him going in circles. He's in the city jail. The others are all chatting with the Devil. Probably negotiating either boiling water or slow-roasting flames."

I tried to smile, but it hurt too bad. Then I asked again. "Where am I?"

"You're in the governor's suite in the Niantic."

"Nice bed," I managed, then added, "I think I need to sleep a while."

"Can't. Doctor wants to examine you, now that you're awake. You took a hell of a whack from that copper's nightstick."

"Is that doc close by?" I asked, as sleep seemed the only thing in the universe at the moment.

He was across the room. He messed with me for a few moments. I sucked down a glass of water, then I felt a pat on my shoulder and things went dark again.

When I awoke there was a young lady in an apron in a chair across the room, and she was tatting or darning or knitting or some dang thing.

"Ma'am," I said, and she jumped like I'd poked her with one of her needles, but she set her work aside and hurried to my side.

"You're awake. Can you see all right?"

"Yes, ma'am, well enough to see you're not an angel, even if you're pretty as one."

She blushed. "You need a drink or anything?"

Now it was my turn to blush. "I need you to excuse yourself. I presume there's a chamber pot under this bed?"

"There is, but I'm to get one of the gentlemen to help you, should you want to get out of bed."

"Ma'am, I've been using the facilities for several years.

Admittedly, mostly rocks and trees and a few privies, so I can manage a chamber pot. Now, if you don't mind."

She hurried out and just as I was buttoning my long John bottoms, all I had on, Lord Stanley-Smyth came in and closed the door quietly behind himself.

"How's the head?" he asked, seemingly with some concern.

"Well, sir, it seems to be right here atop my shoulders as the Good Lord designed. Throbbing a bit but attached."

"The kitchen is bringing you some broth. As soon as you feel up to it, we need to talk."

"No disrespect, sir, but as soon as I feel up to it, we need to settle up and I need to get on my horse. Speaking of my horse, Sandy, my Sand Bay was aboard the Lawrence?"

"In the city's finest livery not three blocks from here. I've had a vet look at him. He's been curried, his feet trimmed, and looks better than you've ever seen him."

I gave him a sincere, "Thank you. I feel good enough to parley, if that's your desire."

"Parley," he said, with a laugh. "All right, young Mister Zane. I'll lead off. All right with you?"

I managed a nod as I crawled back under the covers.

"You've got a fair bit of money coming. Max was, as I mentioned, my stepson, my second wife's son. Matilda was here in the room with us when you came to. The gray-blonde lady over in the corner, if you remember any of it."

"A handsome lady," I managed.

"We've decided to pay you the wages and bonus that this Jasper, Alabama, and Stadt had coming. You said the cook, Chang I think you said, is recovering up in Leodocia. We'll get a draft up to him for his wages and bonus."

I didn't mention I'd already advanced him a hundred dollars, as I'd settle up with the Lord for selling the stock.

He may want that money back. But Chang was worth every penny if it did.

He continued. "Tiny tells me you want to return via Portland up in Oregon territory? Something about a young lady there?"

"Probably married with twins and fat with another set," I said. And we both laughed.

"If you'd like, I'll hire a man in Portland to find her situation."

I shrugged. "I was heading back that way."

"Not quite yet, we hope. Did Max get a decent burial?"

Again, I blushed. "A foot deep, no casket, a few rocks to keep the critters off, and what I remembered of the Twenty-third Psalm. I wish I could have done him better as he was a fine friend, but we were under attack. I've prayed for his forgiveness. He deserved better."

"And we hope he gets it. His mother would like us to find him and get his body back here to San Francisco in a grave with a proper marker. We're of the Catholic faith, and it's very important to her. Do you think you can find him?"

"Yes, sir, I believe I can."

"We'll pay you handsomely."

"Unfortunately, I need to get back to my farm, but the fact is, seems I'm the only port in this storm. We'll be riding back into the teeth of a dragon. Those savages don't seem fond of white folks."

"The fact is, I'm a substantial political donor to our current governor over in Benicia. And Bigler is a friend of mine as well. Waldo, who'll be running against him in this September election is a strong candidate, and Bigler will need all the help he can get—my help. We'll return to recover my stepson with a platoon of California Guard."

"I want to settle up this trip first, sir. I'll want to send a draft to my mother near Lewiston."

"You have nearly nine hundred dollars coming. How about I make it any even thousand to send home. Then for the trip to fetch Max home, another five dollars a day plus a five-hundred-dollar bonus, you get him back here."

It was more money than I thought I'd see in two years of farming, and I admit I was a little awestruck.

"Fact is I want to give Tiny his wages and I promised him a twenty…"

"I'll make it a hundred plus his wages. He broke one of those Duck's arms before they knocked him silly."

"And I'm told Stadt has a spinster sister in Cairo, Illinois. She has something coming as well."

"I'll forward his wages and bonus to her. And I'll still pay you the thousand, presuming you're going on this quest to recover Max."

"One more thing?" I said.

"And that is?"

"I took a glance into the restaurant downstairs. Before they throw me out of here, I don't suppose…"

"Best meal in the house for you and Tiny, soon as you're able. I've got him in a room downstairs, so he'll be ready when you are. In fact, I've invited the mayor and other city dignitaries to come meet you and celebrate your diligence. To be truthful, I'm impressed a young fella like you had the fortitude to march on. Particularly when you had the temptation of the cargo."

"I'm only tempted by honest opportunity, Lord."

"Three days' time, we've reserved the saloon for you, Tiny, us and about fifty of our dear friends here, then the fifth day, you're off on your mission, if you'll oblige us."

"He was a fine friend, so I'll oblige, pay or not, if there's a way to get there safe and back."

"A platoon of soldiers should solve that side of the equation."

I gave him a nod and a tight smile. Then I couldn't help but smile wide as I shook my head. All I had to do now is live though a supper like I've never had, a party like I've never attended, and another couple of weeks dodging arrows between Modoc and Paiute country.

No hill for this stepper, I thought, remembering one of pa's favorite sayings.

Author's Notes

For the sake of geography accuracy as names and places change over time:

As the west changed and aged, and as some of the early explorers and first settlers moved on, many towns had their names changed. Although I write fiction, I work hard to portray accurate history as to what is transpiring in the country and generally as to place. I do create towns. However, if I wrote novels for another hundred years, I could not portray all the towns in the country that have come and gone. I do take the liberty of occasionally adjusting dates to fit my narrative, but not often.

Brownsville: Le Grand, Oregon was first settled by Benjamin Brown. The Grande Ronde Valley had long been a waypoint along the Oregon Trail. The first permanent settler in the La Grande area was Benjamin Brown sometime before 1861. Not long after, the Leasey family and about twenty others settled there. The settlement was originally named after Ben Brown as Brown's Fort, Brown's Town, or Brownsville. There was already a Brownsville in Linn County, so when the post office was established in 1863, a more distinctive name was needed.

It was decided to use "La Grande", a phrase used by a Frenchman, Charles Dause, to describe the area's scenic splendor.[10] Before the post office was established, William Currey charged fifty cents a letter to carry the mail on horseback to and from the nearest post office, in Walla Walla, Washington.[10] La Grande was incorporated as a city in 1865,] and platted in 1868.

Rooptown: Susanville was named after Susan Roop, daughter of Isaac Roop, an early settler.[3] It was first called Rooptown, and the present name was adopted in 1857.[3] The Susanville US post office was established in 1860. Susanville was incorporated in 1900.

Leodocia: Red Bluff was originally known as Leodocia but was renamed to Covertsburg in 1853. It got its current name in 1854. Located at the head of navigation on the Sacramento River the town flourished in the mid to late 19th century as a landing point for miners heading to the Trinity County gold fields and later as a temporary terminus for the Southern Pacific Railroad's northward expansion.

Rancho Arroyo del Chico: The City of Chico was founded in 1860 by John Bidwell, a member of one of the first wagon trains to reach California in 1843. During the American Civil War, Camp Bidwell (named for John Bidwell, by then a Brigadier General of the California Militia), was established a mile outside Chico, by Lt. Col. A. E. Hooker with a company of cavalry and two of infantry, on August 26, 1863. By early 1865 it was being referred to as Camp Chico when a post called Camp Bidwell was established in northeast California, later to be Fort Bidwell.[14] The city became incorporated January 8, 1872. Chico was home to a significant Chinese American community when it was first incorporated, but arsonists burned Chico's Chinatown in February 1886, driving Chinese Americans out of town. Historian W.H. "Old Hutch" Hutchinson identified five events as the most seminal in Chico history. They included the arrival of John Bidwell in 1850.

Ophir City: Oroville is situated at the base of the foothills on the banks of the Feather River where it flows out of the Sierra Nevada onto the flat floor of the Sacramento Valley. It was established as the home base of navigation on the Feather River to supply gold miners during the California Gold Rush. The town was originally named "Ophir City", but was later changed to Oroville when the first post office opened in 1854 (oro is the Spanish word for "gold").[9] The City Of Oroville was incorporated on January 3, 1906.

Captain Chadwick and the steamship Lawrence did work the rivers at that time. An earlier western of mine, Benicia Belle, dealt with the river trade and was a Western Writers of America Spur Award runner up.

Smith's Landing: Antioch, formerly Smith's Landing, is one of the oldest towns in California. In 1848, John Marsh, owner of Rancho Los Meganos, one of the largest ranches in California, built a landing on the San Joaquin River in what is now Antioch. It became known as Marsh's Landing, and was the shipping point for the 17,000-acre rancho. It included a pier extending well out into the river, enabling vessels drawing 15 feet of water to tie up there at any season of the year. The landing also included a slaughterhouse, smokehouse for curing hams, rodeo grounds, and even a 1½-story dwelling, embellished with fretwork, that was brought around the Horn to serve as a home for the mayordomo (manager) and his wife. In 1849, twin brothers, Rev. William Wiggins Smith and Rev. Joseph Horton Smith sailed from Boston, purchased land from John Marsh[16] and founded a town slightly west of Marsh's Landing, and named it Smith's Landing[17]. During the town picnic on July 4, 1851, William, the town's new minister persuaded the residents to change the name of the town to Antioch, for the biblical city of Antioch "inasmuch as the first settlers were disciples of Christ, and one of them had died and was buried on the land, that it be given a Bible name in his honor, and suggested 'Antioch', (a Syria town where two important rivers meet and where the followers of Christ were first called Christians), and by united acclamation it was so christened."

I hope you enjoyed Rugged Trails and, if you haven't already read it, will enjoy the prequel, Two Thousand Grueling Miles. I have many other westerns set in California, Wyoming, Arizona and Montana and hope you'll look for them on Amazon or in your local bookstore, in eBook, paperback, and many in large print hardcover.

OTHER FINE ACTION ADVENTURE
FROM L. J. MARTIN

Two Thousand Grueling Miles. Young but determined, the man of the family too soon, Jake Zane comes of age with the help of a massive mute escaped slave. It's conquer the wilderness, protect your mother and sisters, or die trying.A grueling challenge…2,000 miles of rutted trail with little or no civilization, no water or far too much, wild animals, wicked weather, and savages both red and white. The good news: you have family and friends, and hundreds more making the trip. That is, until disease and accidents threaten everything. The Oregon Trail is the artery that brought lifeblood to the west, long before wagon or rail. It was the ultimate challenge for thousands who wanted land and opportunity.

Shadow of the Mast. When young Sam McCreed is shanghied he awakens aboard a California-bound hide, horn, and tallow brig. A ship he didn't want to join, on his way to a place he thought he'd never see…driven on by a vicious captain and sadistic first mate. By the time they reach the Pacific, Sam is no longer a boy but a young man hardened by ice, sea, and lash. A California that seemed a peaceful land becomes a caldron boiling over with danger and resentment. And Sam McCreed, now an expert with blade, musket, and reata, is a man on the prowl for vengeance…and he'll send any man who stands in his way straight to hell.

Rush to Destiny. RUSH TO DESTINY is based on the early life of the west's most quintessential hero, Edward Fitzgerald Beale. Ned Beale crossed the country horseback 13 times, he was the hero of the Battle of San Pasqual, the leader of the great camel experiment, carried the first evidence of the California gold rush to congress, fought the slave trade, was an Indian agent in California, and so much more. Beale's exploits eclipsed those of Fremont, Stockton, Custer, and even Kit Carson's, who said of Beale, "I can't believe this man, Ned Beale." My finest compliment as an author came from a California high school history teacher who said, "my students learn more California history from your book than from all their texts, ...and love doing it." Don't miss the adventures of this true hero.

Unchained. Jonas Cable is living exactly the life he wants...in a cabin on a lake in Montana. But a letter from a daughter he wasn't allowed to see changes all that in a heartbeat. He has a grandson he didn't know about, and his daughter pleads with him to get the 14 year old boy out of the hood. Does he owe her anything? Can he put up with a bad kid from East L.A.? And why should he change his life for someone he doesn't know and has not heard from in 30 years? And the last thing he needs is to get crossways with the L. A. gangs

Tin Angel. In this rollicking western romance, written by New York Times bestselling author Kat Martin, with husband L. J. Martin, Jessica Taggart, fresh out of a Boston finishing school, comes West...to discover the "restaurant" she's inherited from her late father is actually a saloon and bawdy house! And to add to the insult, it's run by a handsome rogue, Jake Weston, who owns 49% of Taggart Enterprises.

Myrtle Mae & The Crew. Myrtle Mae is the creation of conservative blog author L. J. Martin, and is a humorous look, as well as a serious look, a what's happening in and to our country.

Blood Mountain. One man ruled the mountainside - and made a deal with the would-be railroad's competitors. If Simon Striker could stop the steel tracks, he could earn a fortune. Now a brawling, quarrelling crew of immigrant railroad workers - Chinese, Irish and Polish - are about to be swept into a death trap in the mountain. And as Striker unleashes his landslide of terror, treachery and murder, a tough Irishman and sword-wielding Chinese fighter are going after him - in a battle of courage and cunning on a mountain stained with blood.

Windfall. From the boardroom to the bedroom, David Drake has fought his way…nearly…to the top. From the jungles of Vietnam, to the vineyards of Napa, to the grit and grime of the California oil fields, he's clawed his way up. The only thing missing is the woman he's loved most of his life. Now, he's going to risk it all to win it all, or end up on the very bottom where he started. This business adventure-thriller will leave you breathless.

West of the War. Young Bradon McTavish watches the bluecoats brutally hang his father and destroy everything he's known, and he escapes their wrath into the gunsmoke and blood of war. Captured and paroled, only if he'll head west of the war, he rides the river into the wilds of the new territory of Montana where savages and grizzlies await. He discovers new friends and old enemies…and a woman formerly forbidden to him.

Bloodlines. When an ancient document is found deep under the streets of Manhattan, no one can anticipate the wild results. A businessman is forced to search deep into his past and reach back to those who once were wronged, and redeem for them what is right and just. There's a woman he's yearned for, and must have, but all is against them…and someone wants him dead.

Repairman Series:

The Repairman. No. 1 on Amazon's crime list! Got a problem? Need it fixed? Call Mike Reardon, the repairman, just don't ask him how he'll get it done. Trained as a Recon Marine to search and destroy, he brings those skills to the tough streets of America's cities. If you like your stories spiced with fists, guns, and beautiful women, this is the fast paced novel for you.

The Bakken. No. 1 on Amazon's crime list! The stand alone sequel to The Repairman. Mike Reardon gets a call from his old CO in Iraq, who's now a VP at an oil well service company in North America's hottest boomtown, and dope and prostitution is running wild and costing the company millions, and the cops are overwhelmed. If you have a problem, and want it fixed, call the repairman… just don't ask him what he's gonna do.

G5, Gee Whiz. When a fifty million dollar G5 is stolen and flown out of the country, who you gonna call? If you have a problem, and want it fixed, call the repairman… just don't ask him what he's gonna do.

Who's On Top. Mike Reardon thinks his new gig, finding an errant daughter of a NY billionaire will be a laydown…

how wrong can one guy be? She's tied up with an eco-terrorist group, who proves to be much more than that. And this time, the group he's up against may be bad guys, or kids with their heart in the right place. Who gets lead and who gets a kick in the backside. And if things go wrong, the whole country may be at risk! Another kick-ass Repairman Mike Reardon thriller from acclaimed author L. J. Martin.

Target Shy & Sexy. What's easier for a search and destroy guy than a simple bodyguard gig, particularly when the body being guarded is on of America's premiere country singers and the body is knockdown beautiful...until she's abducted while he's on his way to report for his new assignment. Who'd have guessed that the hunt for his employer would lead him into a nest of hard ass Albanians and he'd find himself between them and some bent nose boys from Vegas! Another in the highly acclaimed The Repairman Series...Mike Reardon is at it again.

Judge, Jury, Desert Fury. Back in the fray, only this time it's as a private contractor. Mike
Reardon and his buddies are hired to free a couple of American's held captive by a Taliban mullah, and, as usual, it's duck, dodge and kick ass when everyone in the country wants a piece of you. Don't miss this high action adventure by renowned author L. J. Martin. No. 6 in The Repairman series, each book stands alone.

No Good Deed. Going after some ruthless kidnappers, who want NATO,s secrets, is one thing...going into Russia is another altogether. But when one of Reardon's crew is being held, he says to hell with it, no matter if he's risking starting World War 3! Why not add the CIA and the State Department to your list of enemies when your most important job is staying alive hour by hour, minute by minute.

Overflow. Mike Reardon, the Repairman, hates to mess his own nest—to work anywhere near where he lives. If you can call a mini-storage and a camper living. But when terrorists bomb Vegas, and a casino owner's granddaughter is killed…the money is too good and the prey is among his most hated. Then again nothing is ever quite like it seems. Now all he has to do is stay alive, tough when friends become enemies and enemies far worse, and when you're on top the FBI and LVPD's list.

The K Factor. When Mike Reardon, known as the repairman for taking jobs outside the law, is invited to a meeting with the CIA, NSA, and DOD, he knows he's about to be downrange of ka ka hitting the fan.
All they want is for him to go into North Korea and extract three women; a daughter and granddaughters of NK's ambassador to China, who wants to defect. Since he's the former head of NK's nuclear program, the U.S. is more than merely interested in him.

The Manhunter Series:

Crimson Hit. Dev Shannon loves his job, travels, makes good money, meets interesting people…then hauls them in cuffs and chains to justice. Only this time it's personal.

Bullet Blues. Shannon normally doesn't work in his hometown, but this time it's a friend who's gone missing, and he's got to help…if he can stay alive long enough. Tracking down a stolen yacht, which takes him all the way to Jamaica, he finds himself deep in the dirty under-belly of the drug trade.

Quiet Ops. "...knows crime and how to write about it... you won't put this one down." Elmore Leonard
L. J. Martin with America's No. 1 bounty hunter, Bob Burton, brings action-adventure in double doses. From Malibu to West Palm Beach, Brad Benedick hooks 'em up and haul 'em in...in chains.

The Clint Ryan Series:

El Lazo. John Clinton Ryan, young, fresh to the sea from Mystic, Connecticut, is shipwrecked on the California coast...and blamed for the catastrophe. Hunted by the hide, horn and tallow captains, he escapes into the world of the vaquero, and soon gains the name El Lazo, for his skill with the lasso. A classic western tale of action and adventure, and the start of the John Clinton Ryan, the Clint Ryan series.

Against the 7th Flag. Clint Ryan, now skilled with horse and reata, finds himself caught up in the war of California revolution, Manifest Destiny is on the march, and he's in the middle of the fray, with friends on one side and coun-trymen on the other...it's fight or be killed, but for whom?

The Devil's Bounty. On a trip to buy horses for his new ranch in the wilds of swampy Central California, Clint finds himself compelled to help a rich Californio don who's beautiful daughter has been kidnapped and hauled to the barracoons of the Barbary Coast. Thrown in among the Chinese tongs, Australian Sidney Ducks, and the dredges of the gold rush failures, he soon finds an ally in a slave, now a newly freedman, and it's gunsmoke and flashing blades to fight his way to free the senorita.

The Benicia Belle. Clint signs on as master-at-arms on a paddle wheeler plying the Sacramento from San Francisco to the gold fields. He's soon blackmailed by the boats owner and drawn to a woman as dangerous and beautiful as the sea he left behind. Framed for a crime he didn't commit, he has only one chance to exact a measure of justice and...revenge.

Shadow of the Grizzly. "Martin has produced a land-locked, Old West version of Peter Benchley's Jaws," Publisher's Weekly. When the Stokes brothers, the worst kind of meat hunters, stumble on Clint's horse ranch, they are looking to take what he has. A wounded griz is only trying to stay alive, but he's a horrible danger to man and beast. And it's Clint, and his crew, including a young boy, who face hell together.

Condor Canyon. On his way to Los Angeles, a pueblo of only one thousand, Clint is ambushed by a posse after the abductor of a young woman. Soon he finds himself trading his Colt and his skill for the horses he seeks...now if he can only stay alive to claim them.

The Montana Series – The Clan:

McCreed's Law. Gone...a shipment of gold and a handful of passengers from the Transcontinental Railroad. Found...a man who knows the owlhoots and the Indians who are holding the passengers for ransom. When you want to catch outlaws, hire an outlaw...and get the hell out of the way.

Stranahan. "A good solid fish-slinging gunslinging read," William W. Johnstone. Sam Stranahan's an honest man who finds himself on the wrong side of the law, and the law has their own version of right and wrong. He's on his way to find his brother, and walks into an explosive case of murder. He has to make sure justice is done…with or without the law.

McKeag's Mountain. Old Bertoldus Prager has long wanted McKeag's Mountain, the Lucky Seven Ranch his father had built, and seven hired guns tried to take it the hard way, leaving Dan McKeag for dead…but he's a McKeag, and clings to life. They should have made sure…for now it will cost them all, or he'll die trying, and Prager's in his sights as well.

Wolf Mountain. The McQuades are running cattle, while running from the tribes who are fresh from killing Custer, and they know no fear. They have a rare opportunity, to get a herd to Mile's and his troops at the mouth of the Tongue…or to die trying. And a beautiful woman and her father, of questionable background, who wander into camp look like a blessing, but trouble is close on their trail…as if the McQuades don't have trouble enough.

O'Rourke's Revenge. Surviving the notorious Yuma Prison should be enough trouble for any man…but Ryan O'Rourke is not just any man. He wants blood, the blood of those who framed him for a crime he didn't commit. He plans to extract revenge, if it costs him all he has left, which is less than nothing…except his very life.

Eye For Eye. They thought his Mexican wife was a squaw…and meant only to shame, but killed instead.

Quint Reagan hung up his badge, sold his ranch, and with a Smith and Wesson Russian, two Colt's, a Winchester and a coach gun went on the hunt. The Triple R had a hundred riders...but he only wanted to tack the hide of seven to the outhouse wall but the powerful owner was one of them. Sometimes revenge is the best medicine for a broken heart.

Revenge Of The Damned. A lie can be a lynchpin for a hell of a lot worse...at times it can end in a lynching! When Linc Dolan returns from the Civil War to find his former commanding officer has lied to his intended about his death in battle, and then married her, it's hell to pay. When a freak early-winter storm finds Linc wounded and sheltered in the cabin of a recently widowed homesteader and her young son, all should be fine...if he wasn't on the run from the law. Now, Bama, a black mule skinner; Twodogs, a Crow tracker; and Dolan, find themselves an unlikely gang. Damned by decent folk, hunted by the law, and pursued by Montana's most deadly man-hunters, they all three are wronged and seek bloody revenge.

The Nemesis Series:

Nemesis. The fools killed his family...then made him a lawman! There are times when it pays not to be known, for if they had, they'd have killed him on the spot. He hadn't seen his sister since before the war, and never met her husband and two young daughters...but when he heard they'd been murdered, it was time to come down out of the high country and scatter the country with blood and guts.

Shadows of Nemesis. When word finally reaches him that his sister and her family have died a horrid death at the hands of a cattle baron and his craven cowhands, Taggart McBain comes down off the mountain with bear traps, a double barrel coach gun, two LeMats, and a Winchester. He's on the hunt. When the task is done and blood soaks the Nemesis, NV desert, he receives a shock—his sister is still alive.

Now, with posters on every trail in Idaho and Montana territories, and a killer's price on his head, he's on the prowl. What he finds is an equal shock, but not so much as to those who hunt him. When the hunter becomes the hunted, there's pure hell to pay.

Mr. Pettigrew. Beau Boone, starving, half a left leg, at the end of his rope, falls off the train in the hell-on-wheels town of Nemesis. But Mr. Pettigrew intervenes. Beau owes him, but does he owe him his very life? Can a one-legged man sit shotgun in one of the toughest saloons on the Transcontinental. He can, if he doesn't have anything to lose.

The Ned Cody Series:

Buckshot. Young Ned Cody takes the job as City Marshal…after all, he's from a long line of lawmen. But they didn't face a corrupt sheriff and his half-dozen hard deputies, a half-Mexican half-Indian killer, and a town who thinks he could never do the job.

Mojave Showdown. Ned Cody goes far out of his jurisdiction when one of his deputies is hauled into the hell's fire of the Mojave Desert by a tattooed Indian who could track a deer fly and live on his leavings. He's the toughest of the tough, and the Mojave has produced the worst. It's ride into the jaws of hell, and don't worry about coming back.

About the Author

L. J. MARTIN IS the author of over three dozen works of both fiction and non-fiction from Bantam, Avon, Pinnacle and his own Wolfpack Publishing. He lives in, and loves, Montana with his wife, NYT bestselling romantic suspense author Kat Martin. He's been a horse wrangler, cook as both avocation and vocation, volunteer firefighter, real estate broker, general contractor, appraiser, disaster evaluator for FEMA, and traveled a good part of the world, some in his own ketch. A hunter, fisherman, photographer, cook, father and grandfather, he's been car and plane wrecked, visited a number of jusgados and a road camp, and survived cancer twice. He carries a bail-enforcement, bounty hunter, shield. He knows about what he writes about, and tries to write about what he knows.

Find more great titles by L. J. Martin and Wolfpack Publishing, here: http://wolfpackpublishing.com/l-j-martin/

CPSIA information can be obtained
at www.ICGtesting.com
Printed in the USA
FSHW011020080120
65840FS